THE
SOME-DAY
COUNTRY

LUKE SHORT

Thorndike Press • Thorndike, Maine

Library of Congress Cataloging in Publication Data:

Short, Luke, 1908-1975.
   The some-day country / Luke Short.
      p.   cm.
   ISBN 1-56054-233-0 (alk. paper : lg. print)
   1. Large type books.   I. Title.
   [PS3513.L68158S4   1992]   92-18230
   813'.54—dc20   CIP

Thorndike Press Large Print edition published in 1992
by arrangement with Kate Hirson and Daniel Glidden.

Cover design by Bruce Habowski, Jr.

The tree indicium is a trademark of Thorndike Press.

This book is printed on acid-free, high opacity paper. ∞

THE
SOME-DAY
COUNTRY

★1★

"Your old man's really tuned up tonight," the big man said.

"Not on your whiskey," the girl said.

"No, my whiskey's made of grain. His is made of hot air with an audience to watch him give out."

This was a sweet-smelling southern Kansas spring night and the year was 1883. Roughly a hundred wagons of all sizes and descriptions were gathered on the prairie, some seventy-five miles east of Arkansas City. The dozens of campfires by the wagons were burning low but the one big fire, around which the wagons' owners were gathered, was big, bright and blazing.

Standing on the bed of a farm wagon drawn up close to the fire was the "old man," Captain Nathan Frane. He had been talking for an hour and planned to talk for another. Nobody but the big man, Will Racklin, the girl, Silence Frane and the Pawnee Indian, Nathan Running Bear Frane, were bored with Cap's sonorous platitudes. The more than a hundred other persons who made up the audience ini-

7

tially had been charmed by his writing and his rhetoric and still were. They were humble people, farmers and their families, and they had just two things in common — a love of the soil and the belief that Cap Frane would lead them to the lands they could stake out and call their own homesteads.

"Now, folks, remember and remember well what I am about to tell you," Cap Frane said. His arms bent upward as each of his huge hands latched around a suspender. He was a big man, paunchy, and the round jowly face below a theatrical mane of long grizzled hair was benign and barely weather-burned.

The gaze from his stern blue eyes shifted from face to face and each man, woman and child had the feeling that he was talking to them personally. "Tomorrow, when we cross the Kansas line and head south, we will be in the territory of our enemies. The first enemy will be the Indians on whose reservation we will homestead. The second enemy will be the Army, who are the Indians' keepers. Like the tribes of Israel, whom Moses led into the Promised Land, we will be hunted, vilified, persecuted."

Nathan Running Bear standing next to Silence Frane said, "Oh, Jesus!" in a tone of quiet resignation.

"Nothing lasts forever," Silence whispered.

"This has," Nathan said. He was a slim young man of twenty-one, dressed in denim waist overalls and cotton shirt. His black coarse hair was cut short and he could have been mistaken for any young farming lad save that he wore moccasins instead of the sod buster's square-toed footwear. He was Cap Frane's secretary, surveyor and body servant extraordinary.

Cap Frane continued, "We will travel in small groups of no more than five wagons. You have all seen and, I hope, memorized the map which shows where we will settle. Choose any route or trail you wish but we will rendezvous on Big Pine Creek."

Nathan whispered to Silence, "It's Big Piney Creek."

"Not any more it isn't," Silence said. " 'The Man' has just renamed it." Silence and Nathan exchanged smiles and then Silence stood on tiptoe and called loudly, "It's 'Big Piney,' Pappa, not 'Big Pine.' "

Cap Frane looked in the direction from which Silence spoke and then he smiled. "We are both wrong, my dear," he said gravely. "The name is Boomer Creek after tonight." He looked around him. "The press of the nation and the people of Kansas have named us Boomers. To them it is a label of contempt. To us, it shall be a name of honor, for we are truly 'boomers.' We believe in 'booming' the lands of this fair country and we will 'boom' out of Kansas and into the Cherokee Strip through the Indians and through the Army to settle our land."

Nathan said again, "Oh, Jesus!"

Many of the farmers turned to see how Silence accepted her father's reprimand. They saw a small slender girl, whose wide-eyed, elfin face in the light of the fire seemed to be blushing. Only Nathan knew that the blush was not one of embarrassment but of shame at the outrageous and pompous sentiments her father had just expressed. Silence's dark hair was worn in a single braid tied with string. The plain cotton dress, over which she wore a man's leather jacket against the chill of the evening, did not hide the already womanly figure of this eighteen-year-old girl.

Because many people were looking at Silence and because he wanted to assert a proprietorship he did not possess, Will Racklin lifted his hand to place it on Silence's shoulder as he called out, "Cap, why don't we name it Frane Creek?"

Swift as a minnow Silence evaded his touch, and while some of the farmers were still laughing at big Will Racklin's discomfiture, from nearby there came a fusillade of gunfire.

Racklin moved swiftly for a man of his towering height and ample weight; he wheeled, drew a pistol from his holster and ran toward his nearby wagons, which were covered by white canvas tarpaulins. He was the only man who moved immediately. The farmers and their families, along with Cap Frane, looked curiously out into the night in the direction from which the shots had come. The big campfire at which most of them had been staring momentarily blinded them.

Almost on the heels of the shots there came the sound of running horses with the accompanying sound of frightened neighing. Too late the farmers came alert as they saw their stock being stampeded through the camp. Behind the last horses were several riders who kept the horses moving by occasional shots into the air.

As these riders passed the assembled farmers, the farmers could pick out separate shouts: "Go home, Boomers." "How's Cap Frame-Up?" "Where are your horses, sod busters?" "Stay away, bib overalls."

Then, as swiftly as they had come, the riders vanished into the night. An angry murmur arose from the farmers as they started to mill and seek out their wagons.

Cap Frane raised both hands and shouted, "Good people, don't panic! Don't panic!" The crowd milled to a halt and now Cap

Frane continued, "I don't think they're stealing our horses because they don't want farm stock. They're only cowboys out to rag us. We'll search for our stock in the morning."

"Shouldn't we go for the marshal?" someone called.

"After we see if there's any stock missing," Cap replied. "Now let's all of us get some sleep."

The crowd slowly dispersed, seeking their own wagons and tents. Cap climbed out from the wagon bed by the dying fire and Silence watched him as he strode directly toward their wagon to which was attached a broad, slanting canvas fly. Nathan already had lighted the lantern. Suddenly, as Silence watched her father, she thought that adversity brought out the best in him. Indeed he had known little else since she could remember. The Frane colonists' departure would be delayed another day or two while their stampeded stock was rounded up but stubbornly and inexorably Cap would move them across into the Cherokee Strip with the faith of a prophet who believed that his will was God's, and everyone knew that God's will prevailed.

It was a soft night, almost electric with spring and Silence did not want to go to bed but knew she must. She made her way past a wagon and ahead of her saw Will Racklin's wagons with their white tarpaulins standing out in the night. She knew why Will Racklin had pulled his gun and run for his wagons. The biggest of the three held nothing but barrels of whiskey and crated boxes of cigars. When Cap Frane's Boomers had settled on the Big Piney and staked out a townsite, Will Racklin intended to set up the community's first saloon. His cargo, precious as gold, was never out of his sight.

Nor was it now. Racklin came out of the shadows and barred Silence's way.

"Nice night, my dear. What's your hurry?"

"I'm not your dear and get the hell out of my way!" Silence said roughly.

"But I want to talk with you." Will's tone held injury.

"You talk to me in daylight and with your hands in your pockets," Silence said flatly.

"This is business."

"With me?"

Racklin moved closer to her and Silence backed off.

"With your dad, maybe. I want to hire his Injun to hunt down my teams tomorrow."

Racklin kept moving closer and Silence kept retreating until her back came up against the sideboards of one of Racklin's wagons.

Then, before Silence could see what was happening, Racklin raised both arms and placed a hand on either side of her, pinning her within his arms.

Roughly then he moved his hands onto her shoulders and his body pressed against hers.

"It took some time," Racklin murmured. "But I've got you now, little hellion."

His face loomed large before her and he moved in to kiss her. Silence ducked her head and her chin brushed Racklin's wrist. Immediately Silence sank her teeth into the base of his thumb.

Racklin let out a roar of pain and snatched his arms away as Silence wheeled and ducked under the wagon.

Hiding behind the big wheel, she wiped Racklin's blood from her lips with the back of her hand. Speaking between the spokes of the wheel, she said viciously, "You goddamn animal, I'll shoot you! I'll shoot you first and then I'll drown you in your own whiskey!"

Cursing, Racklin plunged his arms through the wheel spokes but Silence rolled out of the way and came up on the far side of the wagon. This brought her close to the dying fire of the wagon next to Racklin's.

Shaking with anger, Silence moved over to the fire and shrugged down the sleeve of her leather jacket until it covered her hand. Then she stooped and seized a burning ember, the leather of her sleeve protecting her hand. Then she ran around to the end of Racklin's wagon and threw the burning ember into it.

Racklin, who rounded the end of the wagon at that moment, started to lunge for her, then changed his mind.

"Why, you little —" He never finished. As it came to him what Silence had just done, he vaulted into the wagon bed and Silence, walking away, could hear his loud and rather infantile curses.

At the Franes' wagon, four down the line, she saw Nathan and Cap seated at a folding table under the fly, chatting by the light of a kerosene lamp. Already, because of her youth and temperament, she had dismissed from her mind the scuffle with Racklin. As a youngster growing up near rough Army posts and among rougher men, she had learned to take care of herself. She would not tell Cap about Racklin, but maybe later she would tell Nathan because she needed his cunning help to plot the revenge.

When Silence walked into the circle of lantern light under the flap, Cap looked up and smiled. Nathan was writing something on cheap tablet paper. Silence walked over to her father seated at the table, put her arm around his shoulders and gave him a gentle hug of consolation.

Silence said then, "Well, Pappa, if that's what we can expect from those bastard cowboys, we'd better throw a guard around the camp."

"Silence!" This was one of the numerous occasions when Cap used her name to admonish her, to correct her language and to order her to be still. When, as a younger girl, she had learned the meaning of "silence," she asked her father why that Christian name had been given her. Cap told her that names such as Prudence, Charity and Hope had been given girls to constantly remind them that these were virtues. In her case, Cap said, Silence was especially a reminder since she had cried through babyhood, eternally jabbered as a toddler, argued and fought noisily as a young girl and chattered endlessly as an adolescent. If it was confusing, it was confusing in the right direction, since every time her proper name was used, it was intended to remind her why she had been given it.

"A guard is precisely what Nathan and I were planning against the cowboys whose paternity you just questioned."

"I don't think the stock will drift far, Cap. Those milk cows will calm them down and they never wanted to leave home anyway," Nathan said with some irrelevance.

"I hope you're right." Cap rose. "I'm going

to take my own advice and go to bed. I suggest both of you do the same. We'll all be hunting horses before dawn."

Both Nathan and Silence bade him good night and Cap went out. They heard him climb into the wagon and seek his blankets. Before Silence could pour two cups of the burnt wheat coffee, they could hear Cap's snores. Silence took both tin cups and sat down in the chair Cap had vacated. Somewhere in the camp a dog started to bark and was cursed into silence.

"Should we expect many more of these raids, o mighty Pawnee Chief?"

Nathan grinned and said, "Quit it." He looked closer at her. "Is that blood on your lip?"

Silence nodded. "I bit it."

Nathan threw his pencil on the rough deal table and tiredly leaned back in his chair. "Well, tomorrow's the big day, Sis. You excited?"

"Not any more," Silence said and looked fondly at Nathan. Before Cap acquired this Boomer madness, he had been a sutler in an Army post near the Pawnee Agency; he had nursed the family of a Pawnee scout away on campaign through the usually fatal smallpox. In gratitude the scout named his youngest son, Nathan, after Cap.

Nathan and Silence spent their early years playing, hunting and riding together. When Cap's wife died, Cap took to the trails to spread the same message he had preached in his sorry trading post — the Indians had been given too much fertile land; they could not possibly fill it with their people or cultivate its acreage. This was a country owned by white men who gave it to the Indians and the white man was entitled to homestead it and farm it. Join with him (for a fee), Cap said, and they would move into these Indian lands, stake out homesteads and farm them.

It had been a heartbreaking parting for the two children. Silence, with little schooling, took to the road with her father. Nathan went through the reservation schools and then, because of his brilliant record, was sent to the Carlisle Indian School at Carlisle, Pennsylvania. When he graduated, he came west to track down Cap Frane, not only because he owed Cap his life, but because he wanted to see Silence again. He found that he and Silence were still as close as brother and sister. Behind his rather stolid mien lay a wild and antic sense of humor, which many Indians possessed but which they were very careful to hide from the whites.

"What do you think, Nathan?" Silence asked. "Will it work this time or will it be like all the other times?"

Nathan picked up his pencil and looked at it, then lifted his dark glance to Silence. "Cap never had so many people with him and never so many wagons. Maybe this time he'll get his land and keep it."

Silence sighed. "I get so damn sick of us starting out with high hopes in the spring and winding up right where we began in the fall."

"If you're sick of it, think what Cap must be."

"I know."

"Don Quixote," Nathan murmured.

Silence frowned. "Is that good or bad?"

"Good."

"Is that some more of your college education, Chief?" She could not wholly keep the resentment out of her voice.

Nathan nodded. "Some day I'll tell you the story, I'm too tired tonight." He rose. "Will you kindly get out of my bedroom and let me sleep."

Silence rose, too. "Keep the gun under your blanket, Chief. You may be attacked by a white man."

"I'll keep my ear to the ground," Nathan said, with mock seriousness. "Good night."

It had always graveled Second Lieutenant Winfield Scott Milham that the Army, which supplied its cavalry troops with ammunition for the widest variety of weapons, did not supply shotgun shells for quail hunting. Thus it was that on this evening in late spring, Lieutenant Milham, instead of heading for Fort Reno's quartermaster's stores building, left the officers' quarters and traveled the opposite direction toward the lighted sutler's store just off the Post grounds. He had promised Mrs. Kelso, the commanding officer's wife, a couple of dozen quail for the major's birthday party the following night. As good a shot as he was, he thought immodestly, the eight shells he had in his room would not quite do the job.

A young man of twenty-six, just a few years and two posts away from the military academy, he was tall, lean and mustachioed in the cavalry tradition. As he passed under one of the spaced street lamps, his blue uniform with its tarnished epaulettes had the proper casualness of a young officer who wanted all to know that he had spent time in the field commanding troopers instead of time in the adjutant's office commanding files of reports.

Ahead of him, the stone sidewalk lit by spaced pools of lamplight pointed straight at the huge, two-story frame sutler's post whose ground floor housed Edmond's, with a hotel on the second floor above it. The officers' bar and an enlisted men's bar were side by side next to the store. A wide railed veranda with three separate sets of steps ran the length of the long building and it was the middle set toward which Milham headed. Perhaps fifty barrel chairs were scattered down the veranda which was lit by kerosene lanterns bracketed to the wall. At least half the chairs, especially those near the lanterns, were occupied by idle soldiers, cow punchers sleeping off their liquor and Indians from the Darlington Agency across the close-by Canadian River to the south.

Once his shells were purchased in the big pillared store which held almost every conceivable item of hardware, nonperishable groceries, household supplies and clothes, Lieutenant Milham passed among the scattering of night customers and, through the connecting door, entered the officers' bar.

Because three troops were in the field, the bar was deserted except for Rosey, an aging, shirt-sleeved bartender who was reading a week-old Caldwell, Kansas, newspaper.

However, Milham heard voices from the billiard room in back and he turned right, heading for them and waving carelessly at Rosey who greeted him with a smile that went beyond his professional one.

In the doorway, Lieutenant Milham paused, yanked off his hat, and regarded the two

21

officers playing billiards, one shooting, one watching, both with their backs to him. His weather-burned, bony face, shades darker than his pale, shortcut hair, was saved from a certain homeliness by two startling components: eyes dark as an Indian's under heavy brows that were black and which in no way matched the color of his hair or his full mustache. A look of quiet impudence came into the dark eyes as he said forcefully and crisply, "Attention!"

Neither of the officers even glanced around at this hoariest of military practical jokes. Second Lieutenant Riker Evans made his shot, then looked over at his companion, saying, "Do you feel a draft in here?"

Lieutenant Walker June, without turning, said, "Yes. There's a strange smell riding on it."

Lieutenant Milham smiled, turned his head and called, "Rosey, one double whiskey for me, two glasses of water for my friends." Then he tramped into the room, circled Evans and quietly put his hat and box of shells on the billiard table. He looked solemnly at his two fellow officers and observed, "It's time for you two clerks to get to bed."

This, as Lieutenant Milham knew and intended it to be, was a low blow; both men, bitter but unprotesting, were serving their turns in the adjutant's office. Lieutenant June, swarthy and heavy, looked boredly around this room, which was just big enough to hold the billiard table, several chairs against two walls and a refectory table on which two pleasantly brown drinks were resting. Then his glance returned to the hat and box of shells which were disrupting the game.

He said with mock coldness, "Would you care to remove those, Mister Milham?" He emphasized the Mister, which was the form of address for second lieutenants and which every one of them hated.

Lieutenant Evans, a slight, curly-haired young man barely over the minimum required Army height, added, "And yourself along with them, Mister?"

At this juncture, Rosey came into the room and deposited Milham's drink along with two glasses of water on the refectory table.

"There's money on this game, I presume, gentlemen?" Milham said.

"Ours," Lieutenant June said pointedly.

"May I join you?"

"You could if you were asked," Evans said and looked at June. "Was he?"

"I didn't hear it," June said.

Still unsmiling, Milham reached in his pocket, produced a silver dollar and laid it on the edge of the table. "We'll have a new game, gentlemen, if you aren't too frail to play it."

"We *have* a game," Lieutenant June said.

"Faint heart never won that fair lady on this dollar, Mr. June."

"What game?" Evans asked.

Milham said quietly, "We play billiards, shooting in rotation, but the hat and shells remain where they are. Shoot over them, bank around them, but when the cue ball touches either one, the shooter must drop out and forfeit his dollar."

June looked at Evans and a faint grin touched his broad face. "Shall we humor this child?"

"It's the only way we'll get rid of him."

Milham said swiftly, "I claim first turn."

Without a word, he placed the balls, then, borrowing Evans' cue, he shot gently. The white ball caromed off the cue ball and slowly, inexorably, wound up neatly behind the hat and the box of shells which lay between it and the cue ball.

As the cue ball came to rest, Lieutenant Evans barked, "Attention!"

Not even looking up, Milham said, "Please, not twice in one night."

Evans repeated, "Attention!" crisply. Milham straightened up to look at him and now he saw Evans facing the doorway. Major Kelso, his commanding officer, was standing in it.

24

Kelso was a tall, thick, ruddy-faced man and there was curiosity in his pale eyes as he looked at his three officers standing at attention, then at the table, then back to them.

"Gentlemen," he said, his voice lagging, "why the formality?"

"You walked in on a bad joke, Sir."

"I hope it was a joke. This oak leaf comes between me and a lot of people." He paused. "Scott, will you bring your drink and step into the barroom, please."

Scott followed Major Kelso into the empty barroom. After Major Kelso seated himself at one of the card tables, Scott, still standing, said, "Like a drink, Sir?"

"I would. Make it a triple."

Lieutenant Milham crossed to the bar and waited while Rosey poured half a water glass of whiskey, then went back to the table and set it before Major Kelso. Seating himself, Lieutenant Milham lifted his drink and said, "Your health, Sir."

Major Kelso, lifting his glass, said, "Thank you." A wry smile broke on his face. "I'll need health. I'm forty-eight tomorrow and I'm still a brevet major."

"Not for long, Sir."

"Shall I say we both hope?" Both men drank, then Major Kelso slapped down his glass with such vehemence that it could have been heard in the billiard room.

"I'm in trouble and you inherit it, Scott." He paused. "Didn't you handle Cap Frane and his Boomers a couple of years ago?"

"Yes, Sir."

"You're going to handle them again."

Lieutenant Milham felt a mild dread, but he said nothing.

"He's back in the Cherokee Strip, this time with a hundred wagons."

"A hundred?"

"That's the word I got tonight from a Diamond H rider. Jess Hovey — he's Diamond H — has a lease on graze in the Strip. His men were gathering beef this week and came across Cap Frane's camp on Big Piney Creek. They must have been there at least two weeks. They have a townsite staked out, they're building soddies and they're breaking the land. We have to move them off." He frowned, as if trying to remember something he could not immediately recall. "You moved Cap Frane off the Strip two years ago and that was before my time. How did you do it?"

"Illegally, Sir. There were seven wagons. At gunpoint I rounded up their stock and told them they could pick them up at the Kansas border. That night Cap Frane's daughter came into camp and asked me to return their horses and mules. She said Cap had quit and that

26

he and his Boomers were going back to Kansas if they could get back their stock."

"Think it will work again?"

"How many men will I have?"

Major Kelso said grimly, "Let's say twelve."

"A hundred wagons means a hundred rifles, Sir."

Major Kelso scowled. "You mean they'd fight?"

"I don't think so, Sir, but twelve men can't bluff them. They wouldn't stand and watch us round up their stock."

Slowly Major Kelso finished off his drink, waited a moment to catch his breath and then said, "Scott, I can't strip the post. With two troops in the field, a squad of a dozen men is all I can spare."

Lieutenant Milham knew his dilemma. With B Troop down on the Washita and C Troop at Camp Supply, Major Kelso had a bare housekeeping unit in A, which, like the other troops, was not full strength. For lack of troops the Boomers probably could not be moved. If he waited for troops, then used them, he would be accused of wrecking a well built-up settlement. On the other hand, he must show superiors that he made an effort to halt the settlers from building, and that he ordered them off Indian lands.

A barely audible sigh indicated that Major

Kelso had made up his mind. "Start with your detail in the morning, Scott. Your orders are to try to peacefully persuade Cap Frane to move off Cherokee land. If he refuses you can promise him I'll send enough troops to level their buildings and trample their crops." He grimaced at what he had just said, then went on, "Explain to them that this will make it impossible for them to get through the winter. Tell them they may as well move now, rather than when the snow comes." He paused and added, "Take Private Scolley if you want."

Lieutenant Milham smiled faintly, "Sir, I'm too wise to accept your offer of Scolley. I can't imagine Mrs. Kelso giving a birthday party without an orderly's help." At Major Kelso's nod he added, "Will you tell Mrs. Kelso that she'd better plan a change in the menu? She'll know what I mean, Sir."

Kelso asked gruffly, "Well, what do you mean?"

"I was supposed to get a couple of dozen quail for tomorrow's dinner, Sir."

Major Kelso smiled and heaved himself to his feet. "I'll get them for you, Scott." Now he was all business again. "Draw rations for two weeks for men and horses. Let me know by courier what the situation is after you have talked with Cap Frane. Thanks for the drink and good night."

Milham saluted and watched Major Kelso part the batwing doors and vanish into the night. No formal good-by, no wish of good luck, Milham thought, and why should there be? Of all the sorry assignments he could possibly draw, this was the sorriest. It was a policing job of the lowest category, frustrating in that he probably could accomplish nothing, and even if he succeeded, it would have to be done over and over again, if not by himself then by a brother officer. The Boomers were stubborn and unteachable.

Lieutenant Milham picked up the two empty glasses, tramped over to the bar, put the glasses on its top, said "Mark me down, Rosey," then turned and entered the billiard room.

Lieutenants June and Evans had removed his hat and box of shells from the table.

Milham moved over to his hat as Lieutenant Evans asked, "What was that all about, Mr. Milham?"

"Secret assignment," Milham said curtly.

"Trouble?" Lieutenant June asked.

"Deep trouble," Milham said drily. "I am sweeping a bunch of Boomers over the Kansas line."

Both June and Evans instantly laughed.

"I suppose you're heading back to quarters to write a farewell letter to your girl. Do you want me to ask the chaplain to stop by?"

Evans said gravely, "You may not come through this assignment, you know."

Milham said mildly, "You two clerks can both go to hell."

As he headed for the door, Lieutenant June said mockingly, "Farewell, Caesar," and Lieutenant Milham did not dignify the thrust with an answer.

As he crossed the empty barroom, he was already planning for the morning. He would find Sergeant Macy tonight, go over the names of the detail with him, trying to balance it evenly between regulars and new men. With the squad so decimated, he could not take Macy too, but would take Corporal Byrd instead.

Out on the veranda, he cut across to the steps and headed for the post; knowing what he was facing in the next few days, memory made his thoughts turn sour. He was thinking of his last encounter two years ago with Cap Frane. It had happened about this time of year some miles below and to the west of Caldwell. As Junior lieutenant in Troop A, he had drawn the assignment of driving Cap and his Boomers back to Kansas. At that time, Cap had been a stubborn tinpot Messiah, a born barracks lawyer who claimed rights he did not have for himself and his Boomers. Worse than

Cap, however, had been that gadfly nuisance, Cap's skinny daughter. He tried to remember her name but could not, yet it was that feisty brat, rather than Cap, who had goaded the Boomers into a stubborn anger that had forced him to round up their stock at gunpoint and start out for Kansas.

He wondered if she was still with her father.

She still was, as Lieutenant Milham grimly observed four days later when he and his detail rode into the Boomer camp on the Big Piney. It was a bright spring morning as he signaled his detail to halt short of the camp, folded his hands on the pommel of his saddle and surveyed the Boomer camp in silence. The sound of hammering and sawing came to him in the still morning air. This, he thought, was closer to a town than a camp. Canvas-covered freight and farm wagons were scattered across the plain among rising house frames, and beyond them Milham could see the plowmen urging their teams to break the tough sod. Where the land sloped towards the creek valley, a dozen men were digging into the hill and their soddies were taking form. Wives were helping, with their children playing under the trees alongside the creek. It was as active as an ant hill, Milham thought, and he wondered how so much had been accomplished in such a short time.

To Corporal Byrd, the slim, sober-faced young trooper who had reined in beside him, he said, "They see us, Corporal. Dismount the men, I'll ride in alone."

Kneeing his horse into motion, Lieutenant Milham rode into the Boomer camp at a canter. People stopped their work to stare at him as he passed by; only the children greeted him. A tow-headed little girl in a flour-sack dress directed him to Cap Frane's wagon and tent, and as Lieutenant Milham approached it, he saw Cap's girl, the sleeves of her plain gray dress rolled up, hanging out clothes on a line stretched from a fly pole to the wagon. At the sound of the horse's approach, the girl turned and with slow shock Milham observed that this ugly duckling had turned into something of a swan. Her figure had filled out as had her face, and her dark eyes, with darker lashes, regarded him with instant enmity.

"Oh, it's you again." There was both hostility and contempt in her few words. "Don't bother to dismount. Just ride on through."

Then Lieutenant Milham remembered her name. It was Silence Frane. He doubted she had ever been silent in her life except when asleep.

"Miss Silence Frane, isn't it?" Lieutenant Milham asked.

The girl put her hands on her slim hips, an attitude unmistakably belligerent, "Doesn't the Army have anything for you to do except pick on settlers? You're making a real career out of it, aren't you?"

Lieutenant Milham had been expecting something like this, but he flushed anyway. "I am looking for your father," he said coldly.

"Of course you are. Why don't you leave your message and get on your way?"

Milham ignored this and said, "Can you tell me where I'll find him?"

"I can, but I won't."

At that moment a young Indian dressed in waist overalls, cotton shirt and moccasins rounded the wagon and stepped over its tongue. Silence's glance shifted to him and she said, "The yellowlegs are here, Nathan." To Milham she said, "What have you got this time? Two whole troops?"

Milham said with a vast effort at patience, "If your father is leading these people, I'd like to talk to him."

"Oh hell, let's get it over with," Silence said in disgust. "Go find Pappa, will you, Nathan?" The Indian lad disappeared around the wagon and Lieutenant Milham dismounted under Silence's angry regard. The trouble with a good many women, he reflected grimly, was that they insisted on transforming ordinary relations into intensely personal matters. Two years ago this girl had bitterly berated him for moving the Boomers, just as if he, and he alone, were to blame. Now she was picking up where she had left off then. He lifted his hat and wiped the sweat from his forehead with his right sleeve, aware that the girl was watching his every movement.

"Still stealing stock?" she asked.

"Only on Sundays."

A rich sonorous voice spoke from behind Milham then. "Well, well, if it isn't the same lieutenant." Milham turned slowly to regard Cap Frane. He had put on a little weight since they had last met, Milham noticed. The jowls of that theatrically handsome face indicated that in spite of his poor-mouthing he had not been going hungry. A dozen Boomers had come with him and were watching.

"We've been expecting you," Cap Frane said.

Milham eyed him coldly. "If you have, why haven't you moved?"

Cap Frane chuckled. "Oh no, we're not moving, Lieutenant. If memory serves, the name is Lieutenant Milham, isn't it?"

Milham nodded. "Would you like to hear my orders, Captain?"

Cap Frane scratched his ample stomach

through his sun-bleached cotton shirt and his expression was almost benign as he said, "At your pleasure."

"My orders are to escort you and your company, with all their belongings, to the Kansas line."

"That's kind of you, Lieutenant, but we are not going to move. These Indian lands should be opened to white settlers and we are opening them now." He took his oratorical stance, each big hand grabbing a suspender strap. "These Indians are cultivating only a fraction of their land, while legitimate settlers are starving. Sir, I may tell you that —"

Lieutenant Milham held up his hand and Cap Frane ceased talking, surprised at the interruption. "You may not tell me, Captain. I've heard it all before. I can recite it chapter and verse."

Silence said jeeringly, "Recite it, then."

Milham glanced over at her and said tonelessly, "You are being persecuted by a tyrannical government. You have your God-given rights as an American. The Army is the unscrupulous agent of Indian-loving missionaries and Congressmen. If you are to be moved, the Army will have to carry you." He paused. "What did I leave out?" It was Silence's turn to blush and her eyes were bright with anger.

Cap Frane said mildly, "I think you covered

it pretty well, Lieutenant, especially what you said about carrying us. Which you will have to do, Sir, since we won't go peaceably."

Lieutenant Milham knew he was about to sound pompous, but there was no helping it. "You realize that resistance to the United States Army is insurrection and that it will be put down as such."

"Certainly, certainly," Cap Frane said genially. "Go on from there."

By now a large crowd of Boomers had collected and their number was increasing. Lieutenant Milham could almost physically feel the weight of their hostility.

"All right, I will send back word to my commanding officer of your refusal to move. In due time, more troops will be sent here with orders to destroy your buildings and crops. You will have neither shelter nor food for the coming winter. If you are wise, Captain, you will turn back now and take your company West where there is open land."

"Lieutenant Milham, has the U. S. Army ever been defied before?"

"I seem to remember General Custer was defied."

"Exactly," Cap Frane said grimly. "If you try to move us forcibly, Sir — and I don't mean with the piddling fifteen men you have on the edge of camp — we will fight,

36

Sir. In that event you will get your wish. You can massacre us all."

Milham knew it was time to end this. He had carried out his orders to the letter and it made no sense to stand here any longer exchanging threats with this lunatic. Now his glance roved the crowd; some of the faces reflected anger and some only the stubbornness that had rubbed off from Cap Frane. His glance finally settled on Silence, who had moved to the inside of the loose circle. Her arms were folded across her breasts and there was a look of almost sleepy pleasure on her face as she regarded him. Then he looked at Cap Frane and said coldly, "Good day, Sir." He moved toward the crowd that parted and watched him as he tramped to his horse.

Gathering his reins, he put his foot in the stirrup and started to swing his leg over the saddle. As soon as his weight hit the stirrup, the saddle slipped on to his horse's side and he fell back staggering. Only his reins saved him from falling flat on his back. A murmur of laughter rose from the crowd of Boomers and Milham felt a scalding rage boil up within him. While he'd been talking, someone, screened by the crowd, had loosened his cinch. With quick savage movements Milham tightened the cinch and then lifted his glance again to Silence's face. She, like the rest of these clods, was laughing. She had known about the cinch, which accounted for her expression of sleepy pleasure a minute ago. He would not be surprised if she had done the job herself. Only the Indian lad was sober-faced, as if indicating there was nothing funny to him in watching a man suffer a public loss of dignity. Milham swung into the saddle and slowly pushed his horse through the crowd that was breaking up; then he heard a clear jibing voice, unmistakably Silence's, calling out, "Come entertain us again, Lieutenant."

As he rode back to the detail, Milham's temper calmed and he almost smiled. If he had been a Boomer with a personal hatred of the Army and all it stood for, he would probably have laughed too at a second lieutenant's discomfiture.

Remembering the hostility toward him reflected in the faces of these plain people, he marveled again at their tenacity and their hunger for land. His own family had been Army — his father, grandfather and great-grandfather. His mother's people had been prosperous bankers and merchants in New York State. Not a one of them had wrested a living from the soil except to lend money at interest which went to buy farms for other men. Still, in the West, with little money circulating, land was a form of wealth that would feed a man and his family, and it was no wonder they counted it precious and would go to any end to acquire it. Given other circumstances of birth and training, he could well be one of their number, he thought.

The detail was sprawled in the shade of some pin oaks with one trooper loose-herding the still-saddled mounts as they grazed the rich new grass. The team, still hooked to the supply wagon, was stamping flies, restlessly jangling the harness.

Corporal Byrd rose to meet Lieutenant Milham and take his horse. Lieutenant Milham stepped out of the saddle and handed his reins to the corporal. "After you've turned out my horse, I want you to hunt up a spot where we can bivouac, Corporal. Near the creek, and get upstream from the Boomers."

Corporal Byrd acknowledged the order with a solemn, "Yes, Sir." Milham knew that the corporal was anxious to know how he had made out with the Boomers, but that information would come later when they were bivouacked. The corporal led Milham's horse toward the herd and Milham headed for the supply wagon. The troopers started to rise and Milham said, "At ease," as he passed them. Once at the supply wagon Milham rummaged around for his duffle and, before he found it, Corporal Byrd rode out on his search.

Milham found tablet and pencil, then sought a spot of shade and slacked down, his back against a tree. Major Kelso had ordered him to report on his meeting with Cap Frane and thoughtfully, now, Milham began to write of the morning's events. Cap Frane, he wrote, was both defiant and confident that he could not be moved. When warned that more troops would be coming, he had been unimpressed. The Boomers seemed to be united behind Frane and they were building homes and soddies that would soon form a town. Some land was broken and crops sown. From the morning conversation with Cap Frane, Milham was certain that this detail could not peaceably move the Boomers. He would try again as he awaited further orders.

The report was detailed and the only thing omitted was mention of the loosened cinch. That was a purely personal thing and in good time he would take care of it himself.

He folded the report and sealed it in an envelope, then turned his head and called Trooper Harvey.

The sleeping trooper under the tree was nudged by his companion who said something to him. The man jumped to his feet, straightened his hat and walked smartly over to Lieutenant Milham, halted and saluted. Milham lazily returned the salute and then extended the envelope which Harvey accepted.

"Harvey, draw rations for four days. You're heading back for Reno with this message for Major Kelso. Wait for his orders and don't loaf on the way."

"Yes, Sir," Harvey turned and strode swiftly toward the horse herd, and as Milham watched him, he picked up the sound of approaching horses. Turning his head, he saw Corporal Byrd accompanied by one of the Boomers mounted on a plow horse. He rose as the corporal reined in and dismounted. The Boomer, a square, grim-faced man of fifty, wearing bib overalls and a wide-brimmed black hat, kept his seat.

"Well, Corporal?"

"I found a good spot, Sir. It would suit us fine, but this man says the place is on his land."

Milham looked steadily at the farmer for a moment, then he said to the corporal, "Signal in the horses. We're moving." When Corporal Byrd had gone, Milham said to the Boomer, "Your business, Sir?"

"He told you," the farmer said angrily. "You want to put a camp on my land."

"Correction," Milham said. "It is not your land and we will bivouac on it."

"I staked it out! It's my homestead!"

"It is Indian land and we will bivouac on it."

Now the Boomer was really angry and when he spoke he shouted, "I'll write to my Congressman! I'll write to your commanding officer!"

"You have no Congressman, sir. If you wish to write my commanding officer, direct your letter to Major Charles Kelso, C. O., Fort Reno, Indian Territory. Now, good day to you, Sir."

He stepped past the Boomer's horse and waited beside the supply wagon while Trooper Harvey hurriedly finished drawing his rations. The Boomer sat glowering, then slowly pulled his horse around and said in a surly voice, "Wait until Cap Frane hears about this."

"I can wait." Milham's voice was dry, almost pleasant, conceding nothing. The Boomer whacked his heels into his horse's ribs and got him in motion. Even the Boomer's back, as he rode off, seemed to proclaim outrage. In some obscure way, this evened things up for the morning's earlier events, Milham thought.

The site of the bivouac chosen by Corporal Byrd was an excellent one. While the corporal and a trooper erected his tent, Lieutenant Milham walked down to the creek which held clear water that was not stagnant. Milham glanced across the stream and saw that the land rose gently behind the trees on the bank. On its ridge he saw a horseman, mounted and motionless, watching the Boomer camp. This, Milham guessed, was no Boomer. He was dressed in ranch clothes and faded Stetson and even at this distance Milham could see that his face was weather-blackened. When Milham returned to camp, he found that his tent was up, rear and front flaps open for ventilation. His cot was unfolded and a canvas chair had been set out in front of the tent. Two of the troopers were driving the horses to water while two more were setting up the night's picket line.

Glancing down at the stream again, Milham saw the rider crossing it, coming toward their bivouac.

As the rider approached, Milham regarded him closely. He was a man of about fifty with blue, appraising eyes over a thin, wide mouth. He had shaved recently, a fact in itself surprising for any man in this country.

He reined in, nodded civilly and said, "You the officer in charge?"

"That's right."

"Name's Jess Hovey," the man said. "Mind if I light?"

"Not at all."

Hovey stepped out of the saddle and thumbed

his Stetson to the back of his head, revealing a bald spot.

"You here to move these Boomers?"

Milham nodded and said wryly, "They don't like the idea."

"I could have told you that," Hovey said. "It was my man that carried the word to you people at Reno." Hovey reached in his pocket, produced a lint-covered plug of tobacco and offered it to Milham, who politely declined. Bringing out his knife, he cut a wedge of tobacco and tongued it into his cheek.

"Well, when do you move 'em, Lieutenant?"

"I'm waiting on orders."

"You know this is my land, don't you?"

"I wouldn't say that, Mr. Hovey. This is Indian land."

Hovey looked at him with feigned hurt in his eyes. "But I lease it from the Indians."

"Illegally, of course."

"I pay the Indians good money for this grass. The Army don't care and it gives the Indians some spendin' money."

"But it's not your land."

"Them Indians treat it as if it's mine, so I reckon it is."

Milham shook his head briefly. "Let's get this straight, Hovey. The Boomers are the Army's problem and not yours."

For the first time anger appeared in Hovey's pale eyes. "Not my problem?" He gestured loosely in the direction of the Boomer camp. "There's a hundred Boomer families there. They'll stake out homesteads of over a hundred acres each. That's 10,000 acres of my grass gone under fence. Not only that, there'll be a town right spang in the middle of my lease."

Milham said coldly, "We'll move the Boomers, Hovey, but not on your account."

"Yes, but when? Now? Tomorrow?"

"We'll need more men than my detail."

"But when you get the men, there'll be a town built. Land'll be broke. Then likely the Government will tell them Boomers to keep it. Then where's my lease?"

Again Milham shook his head. "You can't ask the Army to protect you when you're holding land illegally."

"Illegally, hell!" Hovey flared. "Damned near the whole Cheyenne-Arapaho reservation is leased out to cattlemen!"

"But the Army doesn't protect them. If there's trouble, the Army won't help. If a cattleman moves in on a leasee's grass, the leasee's crew takes care of him."

Hovey spat a thin stream of tobacco juice that came perilously close to Milham's foot. "Hell, I can't fight a hundred Boomers. What

45

if I started shootin' them one by one?"

"You'd be in real trouble, I'd say. They aren't trespassing so it'd be plain murder. I imagine the Army would hunt you down."

"They may get a chance to."

Hovey turned, spat again, then stepped into the saddle. Instead of heading back in the direction from which he'd come, he put his horse toward the Boomer camp.

Hovey was a Texan who, for the last dozen years, had trailed herds up the Chisholm Trail to Kansas railheads. Each year he had asked the drover for whom he worked to pay his wages partly in beef. In that fashion he had acquired a sizable herd which he added to by careful thefts from passing trail herds which he and his five-man crew stampeded themselves. He was a tough, imaginative and resourceful man, used to having his own way, and what galled him now was that he was not getting it. His fears that he had related to Milham were genuine. In two weeks, he had seen the prairie broken, hundreds of acres of it, and a town was springing up as fast as men could build it. The Army, he thought bitterly, was helpless to do anything about it, but was too proud to admit it.

He reined in now on the edge of the Boomer settlement, crossed his hands atop the horn of his saddle, and regarded the plowed fields.

46

Most were already planted and greening, he noted, but none of them were fenced as yet.

The beginning of an idea came to Jess Hovey and, touching his horse with his spurs and heading for the stream above the bivouac, he turned it over in his mind.

Suddenly, a few yards ahead of him, a woman broke through the bank brush with an abruptness that startled both him and his horse. Hovey just had time to note the woman was carrying a bucket of water before his attention was demanded by his shying pony.

When he had it under control, he saw the woman had stopped to watch the action. Unlike most of the Boomer women, she wore no sunbonnet and her dark hair was bound loosely at the nape of her neck with a bright ribbon. She was, Hovey saw, on the pretty side of plainness and he judged her to be about thirty. Her blue eyes were watchful and bold and curious as she regarded him, rubbing her hand on the side of her faded print dress.

"I guess I scared him," she observed.

"He'll spook at a bird," Hovey said easily.

There was something friendly in her open manner, a rare quality in a Boomer woman. Then he said, "Looks like some weather might be making up."

The woman looked blankly at the clear sky,

then shrugged. "I don't know. This isn't my country."

"What is your country?"

"Ohio was, but I guess this is now." There was obvious discouragement in her tone. Then she asked abruptly, "Are there any ranches around here?"

"There's some cow outfits."

"Do you know any that could use a cook?"

"That's mostly a man's job in these parts." He nodded toward the Boomer camp. "You got kin there?"

"A brother and his wife. They don't need me and I don't like farming, is all."

Hovey smiled and said, "You're like me." Then he asked, "If I run across anybody wants a cook, who do I say to ask for?"

"Catherine Henry."

Hovey touched his hat at this form of introduction and then the woman picked up the bucket. "I'd best get on. You just tell them my name."

Hovey watched her make her uncertain way across a newly plowed field, heading for a distant plowman. He would like to hire her himself, but he knew that his sorry log shack with its one big bunkroom plus his unwashed crew was no place and company for a woman.

Now he crossed the stream and again his mind returned to the beginning of an idea.

48

☆2☆

Big Will Racklin's Tent Saloon was four wagons away from the Franes', but Silence wished it were four miles. Not that there was any carousing or night hell-raising at his tent; it was because Racklin kept her under surveillance all the daylight hours. Back of his plank bar which rested on two saw horses, he had placed an upright two-by-four to which was lashed a black cotton umbrella. Painted on its side in white letters was the single word, WHISKEY. In its shade Racklin had placed an ordinary saloon chair facing the Frane wagon. Here he sat hour after hour watching Silence wash, make bread, cook and sew. He was, in fact, watching her now.

Will Racklin was a big, loose-faced man with pale eyes and hair as black as Nathan's. His broad hands and splayed fingers had known the plow handle, but not for many years. A sharp card sense had drawn him toward gambling, and for the last five years he had been a reasonably honest house man in a Caldwell saloon. Ever since he could remember, it had been his ambition to own a saloon,

49

even when he was on the farm. To him a saloon owner had money, prestige and influence — three things which he lacked and wanted.

When he first heard the gossip of Cap Frane's gathering Boomers, he was surprised at the number of them. Nothing more. But he could not quite shake the Boomers from his mind. He had seen them wander in and out of the Caldwell saloons, a little uneasy at their town surroundings. They would stretch out a glass of beer for half an hour and they seldom, if ever, gambled because they had no cash money. Yet Racklin knew with a cynicism acquired by working in half a dozen saloons, that, given a hundred men, you would find that fifty of them drank if they had the money. Even a farmer could get tired and discouraged and sick of his woman and his children. A little whiskey helped him forget.

Best of all, Racklin knew, was that if he joined the Boomers, he would have no competitors. Although the Boomers were beer drinkers, he would convert them into whiskey drinkers. Once his mind was made up to throw in with the Boomers, he paid his twenty-five dollars to join Cap Frane's colonists. With money he had won gambling, he bought several barrels of whiskey and crates of cigars. He also bought notions and dress goods for the women. Afterward he hired two teamsters with wagons to haul his goods to Big Piney Creek in company with the Boomers.

So far his plans had worked out well. His tent served as barroom, store and warehouse. The Boomer women hated him for his whiskey but bought his notions and, predictably, the men bought his liquor, by the drink or the pint, mostly after dark.

Right now Racklin was waiting to see what would happen to the Boomers. He made no effort to build anything permanent for his tent would suffice him until he saw whether the Boomers would be moved off or allowed to stay. It seemed to him that the Army could not move off this number of people, but whatever happened, he was sitting pretty.

Except for one thing, of course, and that was Silence Frane. Since the night she tried to burn his wagon up at the Kansas line, she had not spoken a word to him that was not part of a curse. She was a rough-tongued little hellion who only yesterday had drenched him with dirty dishwater thrown from the back of the wagon as he passed. He had left little presents for her in the tent and in her wagon, and found them later thrown out into the walkway or saw them being played with by the camp puppies and children. Still he would wear her down, he knew. She was young, manless, among older men, and this was spring.

Down the rough walkway which was turning into a trampled street, Racklin saw several blue-uniformed troopers coming toward him and supposed they were from Milham's detail. They stopped to chat occasionally with the Boomer children. One lad in the lead pulled up by the Frane tent and Racklin could not hear what he said.

However, he heard plainly what Silence said, which was, "On your way, bub, before I sail this skillet at you!"

The trooper looked startled, backed off a step, then did as he was bid, coming toward Racklin. At sight of the umbrella and its legend, the trooper halted, turned, put his fingers in his mouth and gave a shrill whistle of summons. The other troopers looked toward him, then started to join him. Here, Racklin thought, was some unexpected business, and he heaved his bulk out of the chair and put both hands on the plank, bartender fashion.

As the four troopers moved up to join the first, they passed the Frane wagon and tent. All of them, almost in unison, swiveled their heads to look at Silence, who was working under the canvas fly. The nearest trooper, a tall young man affecting side-burns, lagged behind a step and said something which Racklin could not hear. Then with pleasure but not much surprise Racklin saw a skillet sail from the fly; the trooper ducked and then hurried to join his friends, who were laughing.

The five troopers halted at the plank bar, three of them still joking the tall trooper.

"I sure didn't figure to find whiskey here," one trooper observed.

"I got all you can pay for, gentlemen. You want it in shots or you want to buy a bottle?"

"A bottle," the oldest trooper said promptly.

Racklin reached under the bar and from a wooden box drew out a quart of red liquor which he slapped on the bar, saying, "That'll be two dollars, gentlemen."

As the troopers fished in their pockets for money, the tall trooper kept looking at the Frane tent. Now he looked at Racklin and tilted his head toward the tent.

"What's eatin' at her?" he asked sulkily. "I only said 'You're lookin' mighty pretty this afternoon, Miss.' You'd think I'd said somethin' dirty."

Racklin laughed genially. "They don't love that uniform much around here, trooper."

Before Racklin could scoop up the coins, the cork was out of the bottle and the first trooper was drinking. After gagging and coughing, he passed the bottle on to the youngest trooper, who took it with seeming reluctance.

"What'll the lieutenant say about this?" he asked.

"Hell, kid, we're off duty. He won't say nothin'."

The tall trooper said then, "Let's find some shade and sit down. This whiskey'll warm us up even more."

Together they sought the narrow bar of shade on the east side of Racklin's tent, sat down and took off their hats. From where they sat, the most obvious thing to look at was Silence, who was kneading dough on the makeshift table under the canvas fly.

The sight of her started talk of women and as the bottle passed among them, their stories grew more obscene and untrue. The Boomer women and children who passed them looked away in outrage and disgust; their very attitudes seemed to say that drinking in itself was bad enough, but open drinking was an abomination.

The oldest trooper was the one to finish the bottle, and he held it up, regarding it with something like sorrow.

"That didn't go very far," he mused. "I ain't even got a good start."

In reality he had had an excellent start, as had the others. The combination of the hot afternoon and heavy uniforms seemed to stoke the fire of the raw red whiskey.

Now the oldest trooper said, "Let's get another. What's the sense of drinkin' if you can't feel it?"

"Good idea," the tall trooper said. "Gimme your money."

The youngest trooper and the two others refused to contribute, but the oldest trooper anted his half cheerfully.

When the tall trooper rose, he lurched back against the tent wall, and if it had not been shored up by Racklin's trade goods inside, he would have gone through the tent wall. Then lurching forward he rounded the end of the tent and was brought up against the bar. The sun on his bare head struck him like a blow and he had a hard time getting out the single word, "Another," loud enough for Will Racklin to hear it.

Staggering back to his companions with the new bottle, he sat down next to the oldest trooper.

"Where' res' all the kids?" the young trooper mumbled.

Nobody answered him because the two drinkers were busy drinking and the others were asleep. However, his question started a train of labored thought in the tall young trooper's head. Only the smallest children had spoken to them as they wandered through the camp. The men ignored them and the women turned their backs as if too proud to speak to this scum in blue. Come to think of it, only the girl down the way there had spoken to any of them and that was to threaten Trooper Johnson with a skillet that she had later thrown at him.

"I'll get her to speak to me," he said thickly.

His companion looked at him and when his eyes got in focus, he said, "Who?"

"Girl down there."

"Forget her. It's askin' for trouble if you try."

"I'm as good as she is. Why, I bet she speaks to dogs, but not me."

"Forget it. Have a drink."

"No, no more. Don't want to look as if I was drunk."

He heaved himself to his feet, swayed, fell to his knees, then brought himself upright again. "Too good for us," he muttered and then started toward the Frane tent.

He was perhaps fifty feet from the bar tent when the old trooper called out, "Tom! Come back!" The tall young trooper paid him no attention and now the older trooper heaved himself to his feet and started after Tom. When he was in motion, it was obvious that he was carrying his liquor considerably better than the younger man.

Silence, while not really watching, had observed the drinking which had culminated in Tom's departure. She was aware of his staggering approach but busied herself with her bread. Even when the trooper hauled up by the fly she pretended not to notice his presence.

"Gonna speak to me, Sister? Just say hello."

Silence looked up and said coldly, "Hello. Now get on your way."

"Tha's better. Boomer girl spoke to me." He was talking aloud to himself, but now he spoke directly to Silence. "How come you got mad when I called you pretty?"

As he finished talking, the older trooper came up and halted.

"He bothering you, Miss?"

"Yes. So are you. Get him out of here."

The older trooper put his hand on Tom's arm and said, "Come along now."

Tom wrenched his arm free with such violence that he staggered into Silence before righting himself. "Just answer me," he said doggedly.

Swiftly Silence scooped up a handful of wet dough as she said, "I'll answer you." With that, she plastered the dough in Tom's face.

The tall trooper staggered back a step and then lifted his hand to wipe the dough from his eyes and mouth. At the same time, the older trooper grasped his arm again and swung him around, pulling him off balance so that he fell heavily on his side.

These two incidents of insult were too much for the young Tom. The anger he had felt at Silence's act changed to fury at the old trooper's manhandling of him. Struggling to his feet, he lunged at the older trooper, swinging wildly. The older trooper ducked the swing, then sent a looping blow to Tom's jaw.

The impact of the blow drove Tom backward and he back-paddled desperately to regain his balance.

Silence saw it coming and jumped aside, just as Tom, still back-paddling, crashed into the dough-laden table. It gave way with a splintering crash and Tom sprawled on his back amid the wreckage.

"Oh, damn you! Damn you!" Silence cried.

Tom, with dough clinging to his back, struggled to his feet and lunged toward the older trooper, arms windmilling. They met with an impact that drove the breath from both of them and wrestled savagely before they broke apart and resumed the brawl.

Now Silence watched in furious helplessness as the three other troopers, roused from their stupor by the fight, left the bar tent and came running and staggering toward them.

The youngest trooper was the first to arrive and he made an uncertain effort to pin the arms of the oldest trooper, who promptly wheeled and flattened him with a left to the jaw. When the last two troopers lurched up to the fight, they had no notion of who was fighting whom or why.

They saw Tom jump on the oldest trooper's back; the trooper bent over and Tom went sailing over his head — to land again in the wreckage of the dough-smeared table. This prompted one of the nonfighting troopers to put out his hand to help him up. Tom, rising, thought he was preparing to fight and promptly hit him. This brought the remaining trooper to his friend's defense.

In these moments, Silence saw that all five men were fighting each other. The brawl moved back and forth and finally moved under the fly. A staggering trooper knocked over the cold stove, seized a chair and crashed it down over his companion's head. Then one of the tent poles was knocked down.

The rage Silence felt almost choked her and she looked around at the few Boomer men who had gathered to watch the brawl.

"Stop them!" she yelled. No man made a move.

Suddenly Silence knew what she must do. Cap and Nathan were building their soddy down by the creek and wouldn't be much help even if they were here. Now she ran past a pair of wagons to the edge of camp where their horses were loose in a brush corral.

Reaching her horse, she grabbed a picket rope, hastily fashioned a hackamore and then vaulted up on the horse's back, belly down. Now heedless of propriety, she hoisted her skirt, swung a leg over and straddled him. As she kneed him around, she could hear the brawl continuing.

Now she drummed her heels to get the pony in motion, guiding him with her knees toward the Army bivouac a quarter of a mile away. As she raced across the trampled prairie, her fury seemed to increase with every stride of her horse.

Nearing the bivouac she saw Milham's tent and headed for it. Approaching it she saw him rise from his camp chair, put down a book and look in her direction.

In seconds, she tugged on the picket rope and her horse came to a halt beside Milham.

"Will you come and get your damned drunken troopers out of our camp?" Her voice was shrill with fury.

Milham wheeled and shouted, "Corporal, bring four men to the Boomer camp!"

Then Milham turned, put both hands on the rump of Silence's horse and vaulted up behind her. With a perfectly natural gesture, he put his arms around her waist as he touched spurs to put the horse in motion.

"What happened?" he asked.

"They're stinking drunk and fighting!" Silence said furiously.

The horse, with his double load, labored valiantly at the run back to camp. As Silence rode up to the Frane wagon, Milham knew all he needed to know. The fly was on the ground and under it two figures seemed to be wrestling. Troopers Ryan and Bristol, the tall young trooper, were slugging exhaustedly at each other. Both men's faces were bloodied and cut. Young Thompson, out of the fight, was sitting on the ground nursing a bloody nose.

Milham slid back over the horse's rump and ran toward the two erect troopers, bawling in an angry voice, "Attention!"

His order had no effect on the drunk and bloody pair. Running toward them as they were locked in exhausted embrace, Milham lowered his shoulder and drove into them. Both troopers, weary and caught off guard, toppled over and sprawled on their backs.

"Attention!" Milham said sternly.

Ryan and Bristol looked stupidly at him, not recognizing him, but perhaps remembering the voice. Only Trooper Thompson came immediately to attention; the other two came slowly and painfully erect and stood weaving on their feet, their breaths coming in great, gagging heaves.

"Thompson, get that canvas off those men!"

The young trooper did as he was bid. When he pulled back the canvas he revealed the two troopers lying face down. One had his arm across the other's shoulders as if in friendship. Both men, brawling in the oven heat under the canvas, had lost their fight to whiskey.

Milham surveyed the wreckage and then looked at his sorry troopers. "You're all under arrest," he said flatly.

Now the handful of Boomers watching moved a little closer. Silence was still mounted, watching the scene with anger and disgust. Milham heard the sound of galloping horses now and presently Corporal Byrd and four troopers reined in beside Silence.

"Corporal, these men are under arrest. March them back to camp." He gestured toward the passed-out troopers. "These two you'll have to pack." He looked at the four mounted troopers. "Wilson and Carmichael, you stay and clean up this mess."

"Dismount and load them on my horse and Bailey's," Corporal Byrd said.

Wordlessly, Silence kneed her horse around and rode him back to the spot where he had been picketed. Her rage had raveled out into bitter, angry resentment against Milham. No

officer worthy of his rank would tolerate conduct like this in the men he commanded.
Could it be that in his hatred for her father
Milham had put his men up to this wreckage
and destruction? Immediately, she felt ashamed
of even having this thought. Still, a long time
ago, he had taken Boomer horses at gunpoint,
she remembered.

After wiping down her horse and watering
him, Silence walked back to their wagon. She
arrived just in time to see the tail end of the
procession heading back toward the Army
bivouac. The two unconscious men, belly
down behind the saddles, were being held by
their belts to keep them from falling. The upright three trotted along ahead of the procession. Already the tent fly was up and the
stove had been set upright and the stovepipe
connected. Milham and the other two troopers
were trying to reassemble the table and were
not making much of a job of it.

Catching sight of Silence, Milham came off
his knees and met her in front of the Frane
wagon.

Silence sank down on the wagon tongue.
She was tired and in no mood to receive the
apologies she was sure were coming.

"Miss Frane, that was inexcusable, and I
apologize."

"It was," Silence said curtly, and then she

lifted her glance to regard him. "What beats me is why you let them get away with it. Why did they come here except to do just what they did?"

"I don't think they knew there was liquor in camp. I'm sure I didn't."

"They headed for it like homing pigeons," Silence said tartly.

"I think they were only curious and friendly. Like all soldiers, they're attracted to children and girls. They asked me if they could visit here, since there was nothing for them to do in camp. I planned to let them take turns, a few at a time, so they could meet and know you folks. They are," he added wryly, "human beings in spite of the uniform they wear."

"If it's human to get drunk, fight and insult women, then I guess they are." Perversely Silence suddenly found she was enjoying herself. Somehow Lieutenant Milham's red-faced embarrassment and humiliation was nothing short of poetic justice. The Army had humiliated the Boomers time and again, and now the shoe was on the other foot.

"I wonder if your commanding officer will think they're only human beings when he reads what they did." She paused. "Tell me, will you get a reprimand after your commanding officer reads Pappa's letter?"

"I will." Milham's tone of voice, even his

expression, was formal.

Now Silence smiled for the first time. "Good. Oh, good. That's worth losing a week's bread."

At that moment they were interrupted by Trooper Bailey. "Sir, I reckon if we had the tools in the wagon repair box, we could fix the table."

"Can you and Carmichael pack it between you?"

"Yes, Sir, we'll each take a half."

"Then go ahead, and return it as soon as it's fixed."

Now Milham turned back to Silence. He regarded her thoughtfully. Then he reached in his pocket and drew out a silver dollar. "Would you say this would cover the flour that was wasted?"

Silence looked at the coin, then at Milham. "Why should you pay? You didn't ruin the bread."

"Oh, they'll pay," Milham said grimly. "They won't pay in money, but in other ways. Will you take this?"

"The flour isn't worth it."

"Then buy a fancy for the trouble you've been put to."

Silence shook her head in negation. "No, I won't be beholden to you or the Army. Besides, I've been paid back."

Milham frowned. "How's that?"

Now Silence stood up to her full five-feet-two and looked in Milham's eyes. She had to tilt her head back to do it. "I've always thought the Army regulars were a collection of criminal stable boys. I've thought the officers were incompetent bullies. It's worth losing a little flour to see it proven."

Silence brushed past Milham, leaving him standing there looking at the dollar in his palm. All true, he thought. His troopers were drunks. He himself had acted with the utmost incompetence. As for being a bully boy, he thought grimly, he would see what he could do about that.

As he tramped past the fly, he remembered Carmichael pointing out the tent bar down the line where his troopers had bought their whiskey, and now he headed for it. At his approach, Racklin, who had watched the fight and its aftermath from his chair, rose.

Milham regarded him for a long moment, and then said politely, "Your name, Sir?"

"Will Racklin." Suspicion crept into his face, and he said, "What you want it for?"

"Just to get acquainted."

"Sure," Racklin said derisively. "You don't like me gettin' your sojers drunk, do you. Well, who you goin' to report it to?"

Milham casually began to strip off his blouse as he said mildly, "Report it? I hadn't thought

66

about it. I'd like a glass of whiskey, a big glass." He finished stripping off his blouse as Racklin reached under the bar and came up with a water glass and a bottle of whiskey.

As he set them on the plank bar, he said, "I know my rights, Lieutenant, and I know yours, too. I can sell whiskey to anybody that ain't a kid. I can even sell it to them, but I don't believe in it. You got no authority over me. If you don't want your sojers gettin' drunk, tell 'em to stay away from here. But if they come, I'll sell to them."

"Sure you will." As Milham put down his blouse alongside the bottle of whiskey, he observed, "Hot, isn't it?"

Since the lieutenant seemed to acknowledge the rights involved without argument, Racklin relaxed. He agreed it was hot and would get hotter later.

As he talked, Milham opened the bottle, poured, then raised the water tumbler to his mouth and took a sip of whiskey. Then he turned his head aside and spat it out. Looking at Racklin, he said, "That's the worst whiskey I ever tasted," and without waiting for Racklin's protest he threw the glass of whiskey in Racklin's face.

Racklin backed up, cursing, bringing both hands up to wipe the whiskey from his smarting eyes and face. He was swearing in a strangled voice.

While he was wiping off the whiskey with his sleeve, Milham poured another glass and now Racklin found his voice.

"That's again' the law, the Army doin' that to a man! You know damned well I'm in trouble if I fight you."

"Do you see any Army insignia on me, Racklin? I'm out of uniform. I'm not protesting as an Army man. I just don't like your whiskey. I'm a customer and I've got a right not to like it."

He picked up the second glass of whiskey and threw the contents again in Racklin's face. This was too much for Racklin, who was perfectly willing to accept Milham's trumped up story that he was only acting as a dissatisfied customer. Then Racklin would treat him as one.

Racklin ducked under the bar and came to his feet on the outside of it. "All right, my fine, dandy customer," he growled, again wiping his face with his sleeve. "If you don't like my whiskey, say so. Don't throw it at me."

Raising his fisted hand, he moved his big hulk toward Milham. He got in the first swing, which Milham chopped aside. It left Racklin's whole midriff exposed. Milham planted a left in Racklin's solar plexus which doubled him up in midswing. Then Milham drove a clean hard blow to the point of Racklin's jaw.

Racklin fell over on his back, his arms hugging his bent knees in an effort to gag in air. Milham watched him dispassionately, not even breathing hard, as Racklin fought for breath and finally found it. Racklin's legs slowly straightened and he lay on his back looking at Milham with surprise. Milham went up to the bar, picked up his blouse and shrugged into it. Slowly, painfully, Racklin came to his feet.

Milham placed a silver dollar on the bar and then regarded Racklin.

"If you're smart, Racklin, you'll sell my men a limit of four drinks apiece, then close the bar. No bottles, or I'll be back."

"You'll be looking down a gun barrel when you do."

"It won't be the first one I've looked down," Milham said. He turned and started down the walkway toward the Frane wagon. Silence, he could see, was standing under the fly, her arms folded across her breast, watching him.

As he passed her, Silence said scornfully, "What did that get you?"

"Exercise," Milham said drily, and walked on.

Jess Hovey was wakened by the rain long

before dawn. He decided he'd had enough sleep so he rolled out of his bunk, lighted the lamp on the big bunkhouse table, moved out to the adjoining kitchen shack and built a fire. Afterwards, he came back to his bunk and pulled on a pair of levis and shirt over his long underwear, then strapped on his shell belt.

He'd heard no thunder with the rain, so maybe his herd that was being driven by his crew to Fort Reno had not been stampeded. Now he looked about him, momentarily at a loss for what to do. The cook was with the round-up chuck wagon and his crew of four men were trailing the herd. It would, he reckoned, be about at the headwaters of the Big Piney by now.

Breakfast was a matter of reheating yesterday's coffee and gnawing on some four-day-old pan bread. As he ate standing up in the small kitchen lighted by a bracket lamp, he reviewed his visit to the Army's camp yesterday, and the old anger touched him again. The Army wasn't going to help him against the Boomers because it plain wouldn't and couldn't. A man was taxed to support a bunch of saloon riffraff who were afraid of farmers. Well, that left him to his own devices and he thought he had a device.

Finished eating, he took down his slicker

from a wall nail and shrugged into it, then blew the lamp and stepped out into the rain. Once in the sod barn that adjoined the corral, he lit a lantern and opened the door that led into the corral. Five horses were huddled together under the roof overhang that kept off the rain and snow. In a matter of minutes, Hovey had a horse saddled and was heading north in the graying dawn.

By midmorning he had skirted the Boomer camp where the continuing rain had stilled much of the activity. Three miles beyond he topped a rise, then reined up. Ahead of him he could see a herd of cattle strung out and coming towards him. These would be his three hundred two-year-old steers that the Army at Fort Reno had contracted as beef issue to the Indians. Hovey could see the yellow-slickered riders on point, swing and drag.

He had been spotted, for now his foreman, Yancy Bates, riding point, lifted his horse out of walk and came toward him. Hovey rode to meet him and later both men reined up.

Yancy Bates was a man in his middle thirties, stocky and wide; his broad face was bear-stubbed, and rivulets of water were running off his chin.

"Where's the wagon, Yancy?" Jess asked.

"Downstream a ways from the Boomer camp."

Hovey nodded. "Well, you might as well cross them over the creek here."

Yancy frowned. "I figured to stay this side of the creek away from that Boomer stock, Jess."

Hovey shook his head. "Cross them here, Yancy. Let's tell the boys."

Yancy looked at him with wonderment, then shrugged.

"Once they're crossed, call the boys together."

He and Yancy rode toward the herd and now Yancy pulled ahead as Hovey followed at a more leisurely pace. Aside from the timber on the creek bottom, Hovey noticed there was little else but grass, wild plum and jack-oak thickets to break the rolling and now drenched prairie. Visibility in the rain, he observed, was limited.

He watched the cattle being pushed across the creek and when the last straggler had forded the stream, the four slickered hands collected on the opposite bank.

Hovey pushed his horse through the alders and rode up to them, nodding a curt greeting. Then, as they listened in silence he gave them their orders.

The rain had halted most of the work in the Boomer camp. Cap Frane and Nathan were catching up with correspondence to Congressmen and to prospective colonists. Cap had already completed his letter of outrage to Major Kelso regarding Milham's negligence in allowing his drunk troopers loose upon the camp. Other Boomers were patching harness or doing inside work until the rain let off.

Silence, under the fly, was preparing the noon meal, and was as close to pouting as she ever got. All morning she and Cap had been jangling. Nathan was going to Fort Reno to deliver Cap's letter and Silence wanted to go with him. Cap had refused on the grounds of propriety.

"Pappa, you make me sick. You really do. I've grown up with Nathan and everybody knows it. We've camped out together lots of times."

"When you were children."

"Hells bells, we've wrestled and swam naked. Now all of a sudden you think —"

Silence stopped talking because Nathan had raised a hand. His head was turned in listening. Then he rolled out of his chair and put his ear to the ground, listening. After a moment, he rose swiftly and looked at Cap.

"I don't know what it is, but there's a lot of stock running."

Both men moved over toward their jackets

on the bench, then moved out from under the fly into the rain. Silence grabbed her leather jacket and followed them.

Nathan halted and listened, then said swiftly, "I hear cattle bawling." He pointed to the northeast, and then broke into a run, Cap and Silence following after him.

When they were past the wagons and half-finished buildings, Nathan halted abruptly and pointed. There, to the north, was a stampeding herd of cattle coming toward camp. Already they were in the planted fields, trampling the beginning crops into the deep mud.

From the camp it looked as if punchers were trying to turn the herd and get it milling, since they were waving slickers and shooting into the air. But each time they succeeded in turning the herd, it was into another plowed and planted field.

The gunshots brought the Boomer men at a run and when they saw what was happening, some of them started running across the fields toward the running cattle. Others ran back to their wagons for weapons and mounts. In a matter of minutes all the Boomer men and most of the older children were running or trotting toward the fields.

Now Silence lifted up her skirts and started to join the others.

"Silence, come back here!" Cap bellowed.

"You'll be trampled!"

Silence pretended not to hear and now Nathan took out after her, running effortlessly. Cap, resigned, started plodding toward the fields, too.

The mad and apparently aimless cattle moved from one unfenced field to the next. Just as it appeared that Hovey's hands had succeeded in getting the cattle to mill, so would the cattle be guided skillfully by shots and waving of slickers to new destruction away from the approaching Boomers.

When it appeared there was no more planted ground to trample, the herd was turned toward the Boomers and their camp. Nathan, reading the intent of the trail hands, grabbed Silence's hand and they turned running toward the creek away from the camp.

In moments the herd, harried by the shots and the whooping of Hovey's hands, pounded past them, heading straight as an arrow for camp.

"Oh, Lord!" Nathan groaned. "Those women and kids."

Appalled, they watched the cattle approach the camp. Now the Boomers were shooting into the herd leaders, some of whom were hit and downed. But the smell of blood only increased the terror of the maddened and bellowing steers.

Now Silence and Nathan could see women and children of the camp fleeing out of the path of the oncoming herd before it reached the camp. When it did, wagons were bowled over and building frames were toppled. It took only minutes for the herd to cut a swath of destruction through the camp and vanish into the creek bottom. Several wounded steers were on the ground struggling for a foothold on the wet grass.

Now the Boomer men were hurrying back to see what further damage or death the steers had caused in the camp.

"Oh, Nathan, they planned that!" Silence said miserably.

Before Nathan could answer, they heard footfalls of a horse approaching behind them. Turning, they saw Lieutenant Milham riding toward them, his black poncho glistening with rain.

Pulling up his horse, he nodded gravely. "Was your father in camp?"

Nathan turned and lifted his arm and pointed to the distant figure of Cap. He was standing alone, looking off toward the ruined fields. Across them a lone rider was approaching, his horse at a walk.

Silence brushed her dripping hair from her face. "It looks like Pappa is waiting for him."

"I think he is," Milham agreed.

Without speaking, they headed for Cap who was standing bareheaded in the falling rain. Approaching him and seeing how drenched he was, Silence shivered, perhaps in sympathy. For the first time she could remember, he looked utterly defeated; his shoulders seemed bent under some unbearable burden.

As they approached, Cap heard them and turned. When they halted, he lifted his arms and pointed to the fields and addressed Milham.

"Those were life-giving crops, young man. Yet you and your men stood aside and watched them destroyed."

Milham sat in silent patience, not even bothering to answer. He was watching the rider approaching them.

"Why, it's that Hovey," Silence said, then added swiftly, "Those were his cattle then."

"They were his brand," Milham agreed.

Now Hovey approached and reined in, regarding each of them separately with his cool, appraising glance. He nodded once and lifted his reins as if to ride on.

"Sir, you plotted that!" Cap said wrathfully.

Hovey waited a moment before answering and then he said with heavy irony, "If I did, I'm the first cattleman that ever plotted a stampede."

"You're a goddamn liar," Silence said coldly.

Hovey looked shocked for the briefest moment. Then he said with grave bitterness, "That stampede'll run twenty pounds off every steer — the ones your people didn't shoot, that is."

"Exactly what happened?" Milham asked.

"Crack of lightning."

Silence said, "Or a gunshot. Which?"

Now Hovey folded his hands atop his saddle horn and regarded Silence coldly. "Lady, I ain't afraid of anything in this world but a stampede. They cost lives and tallow." Then he asked bluntly, "Why do you care?"

For a moment — but only a moment — Silence was speechless at the man's gall. Then she found her voice. "Why do I care! Look at the crops your cattle trampled! Look at how they wrecked our camp! You don't know if people weren't killed!"

"Did anybody invite you people on my lease?"

When nobody answered immediately, Hovey continued in his soft Texas drawl that was anything but mild. "Any of you pay the Indians for this land? If I have an accidental stampede on my graze, that's my hard luck. Why were you and your wagons in the way of it?"

"Because you aimed it at us!" Cap said angrily.

"I got a right to do that, too." Hovey looked at Milham. "That right, Lieutenant?"

"None of you have any rights here."

"Except what we can hold. Remember telling me that?" Hovey's tone was sly.

Silence, standing alongside Milham, who was still mounted, looked up swiftly at him. "You told him that?"

Milham nodded. "Yes, when he asked me to shove you off his grass. I told him that down on the Cheyenne-Arapaho reservation there were grass leases, too. If two outfits quarreled over the grass, it was their affair, not the Army's."

"Then whoever is the strongest wins?" Silence insisted.

"You could put it that way."

Cap Frane, on Milham's left, was shivering in the cold rain; he was not about to accept this judgment without protest. He was so cold and miserable that his voice quavered when he spoke. "You are supposed to protect United States citizens, not throw them to wolves like this man."

As he was talking and Milham was watching him, Silence reached under the skirt of Milham's poncho to his holstered pistol, which was tied down to his thigh. Gently lifting it out, she wheeled away from his horse. Too late, feeling the theft, Milham tried to grab his gun and failed.

Now Silence, cocking the pistol and holding it in both hands, raised it, pointing it at Hovey.

"Whoever's strongest, eh?"

Nathan, standing alone on Silence's right, had been watching Hovey and saw the startled expression wash into his face. As Silence spoke, Nathan looked at her, then lunged for the pistol. His hand batted it just as Silence pulled the trigger. A clod of mud erupted under the belly of Hovey's horse, who promptly reared.

Both Nathan and Milham were on Silence now, Milham pinning her arms as Nathan wrenched the gun from her hand. Milham could feel her shivering under her leather jacket, whether from cold or anger he didn't know, but he was sure it wasn't from fear. Hovey's horse was dancing now.

"You idiot!" Nathan whispered.

"I wish I'd killed him!" Silence said slowly. "I do."

Milham spoke over Silence's head. "You'd better ride out, Hovey. If you don't want more of this, you'd better circle the camp, too."

Silence began to struggle to free herself and now Milham released her. Immediately, she looked around for something to throw at Hovey, but he was taking the hint. His horse was already in motion and he was heading for the creek, away from the camp.

When he was gone, Silence turned and saw Nathan in the act of returning Milham's gun. Milham looked up and their glances met.

"I wish I could figure you," Silence said slowly. "You as good as told him to do this."

"I sort of backed into telling him I wouldn't help either of you." This was a correction only for the record, Milham thought dispiritedly.

"Come," Cap said simply. "Let's see what damage is done."

Silence and Nathan joined him and the three of them headed back to the camp without giving even a simple good-by. Milham had intended to ride into the Boomer camp and also view the damage done, but if Cap and Silence believed he had given tacit permission for Hovey's rampage, they would communicate it to the others, and the relations between the Boomers and his command would worsen. *If that's possible,* he thought wryly.

As he rode back to the bivouac his mood was gray and dismal and had nothing to do with the still-falling rain.

Reviewing his handling of this Boomer assignment, he could name nothing of which he could be proud. Mentally, he ticked off his failures: he had been unable to move the Boomers and had been humiliated in the bargain; troopers under him had been guilty of gross misconduct for which he must assume responsibility; and while he had not told Hovey in so many words that he could harass the Boomers without fear of reprisal, he had planted the seed of the idea.

Added to all these failures was his failure to anticipate Hovey's intention to wreck the Boomer camp in addition to destroying the Boomer crops. He should have called out his detail at first sight of the stampede and put it between the cattle and the camp.

But worst of all, and by far the most humiliating, was that he had been disarmed, his weapon taken from him. And by a woman. *No, not a woman, a girl,* he thought. *Not a girl either. A beautiful little fiend.*

He wished passionately that Trooper Harvey would come back with orders to return the detail to Reno. His detail was accomplishing nothing here, nor would they, until they were joined by the rest of the troops. He and his men were totally ineffective, and frustrated to a man.

For the first time in his life Lieutenant Milham wondered if he had the stuff of which an officer was made.

★3★

The rain let off in late afternoon and Cap immediately called a council meeting for the evening. The seven steers killed by Boomer guns had been butchered out and the meat distributed evenly among the families whose wagons containing their food were wrecked, except for one beef that would be roasted for the supper before the council meeting. The Boomer men were already repairing the stampede damage even as the spitted beef was cooking.

But what ordinarily would have been a festive occasion was anything but one this evening. The Boomer men had carefully surveyed the damage to their crops and it was almost total. Those who had broken ground and sown first suffered most, and they would have to replant. Many fields would have to be plowed again.

The grim atmosphere at the big fire was oppressive. The men discussed their misfortune and the women talked bitterly of their overturned and wrecked wagons and of the broken leg suffered by little Willie Madden when he was pinned under a wagon.

Will Racklin, whose tent had been spared, was doing a surprisingly good business. Because their spirits needed lifting and because whiskey might help fight off colds brought on by an afternoon in rain-soaked clothes, the Boomer men recklessly patronized the bar.

When supper was finished and the council was called to order, it was late. Will Racklin's kerosene flare above the bar competed with the light of the big fire. Once again Cap Frane stood on a wagon bed; once again he indomitably tried to raise the spirits of his colonists.

Nathan, however, was not among the audience. Seated on the hinged tailgate of the Frane wagon, which could be used either as a step or seat, he was morosely watching a pair of Boomers at Racklin's tent bar. The kerosene flare, its flame shifting with every vagrant breeze, sent the shadows of the men into a strange sort of dance.

Nathan knew almost by heart what Cap was saying. After invoking God's help, he would get down to particulars. They must obtain seed, he would tell them. If they didn't want a repetition of today's events, they must fence. Proper steps would be taken to prosecute Hovey. (Doubtful, Nathan thought.) Then the eternal discussion of where the money for fence and seed was coming from.

Nathan understood Cap, but he was beginning to wonder if he understood himself, after today's events. Why, for instance, had he interfered in Silence's attempt to shoot Hovey? It was a natural and desirable thing for her to do. Hovey needed shooting, and what more appropriate time and place than here and today. Had he lived so long with white men that he had accepted their form of justice? Nathan wondered.

He could scarcely remember his Pawnee father, but he was certain that his father or any member of his tribe, given Silence's oportunity, would have killed Hovey. If their crops had been wantonly destroyed, the clan (Weren't the Boomers a clan?) would hunt down and kill the destroyers. That was the simple law of life and no Old Testament was required to sanction it.

Objectively now, he wondered what could be done to even the score with Hovey. He himself hadn't been hurt or harmed, but his adopted clan had.

His musing was interrupted by Silence. Quietly, she rounded the back of the wagon and without speaking sat down beside Nathan on the tailgate.

Presently she said, "Woe unto us, Pappa says."

"Because we're sinners?"

"Because we have little faith in the Lord."

Nathan said nothing. After a moment of quiet, Silence said, "Thanks for knocking that gun down."

"I'm sorry I did it."

Silence looked at him. The distant flare barely lighted his dark and somber face.

"I guess I really am, too," Silence admitted. "I wish I could have hit him in the leg, or killed his horse."

Nathan only nodded and now Silence glanced over at Racklin's bar, where a handful of Boomer men were buying drinks. Nathan noticed that the wet weather had put a wave in Silence's hair which made her even prettier in his eyes. Again, balancing his Indian heritage against his acquired white man's tastes, he supposed he should prefer straight dark hair in a woman, but he didn't.

Silence stirred. "I wonder why so many of the men are drinking tonight."

"Trouble."

"I've never believed that."

"Then why do all Indians like whiskey?"

"Fire water, Chief. Remember you're an Indian." Nathan grinned, but said nothing. "You mean Indians always have troubles?"

"They have the white man, don't they?"

"So do we. Like Hovey." She added irrelevantly, "I wonder what it tastes like."

"You've tasted it. Remember that drunk buffalo hunter behind Cap's store?"

"That doesn't count. I spit it out. But what does it taste like?"

Nathan rose. "Want to find out?"

"You're not going to buy me a drink. You haven't got the money."

"Who said I'd buy it?" Nathan stepped into the wagon, rummaged around and climbed down, a tin cup in his hand.

"What are you up to?" Silence asked.

"Injun trick. Come on."

Nathan walked across the road toward the opposite wagon, and Silence followed. They rounded its rear, then turned left. At the back of Racklin's tent, they halted. When Silence said quietly, "Let me come with you," Nathan knew she had guessed. He nodded, knowing she couldn't see him, but also knowing she'd come even if he said no.

They could hear Racklin's voice in conversation with his customers, and this pleased Nathan. He knelt, then flattened himself, lifted up the back of the tent and squirmed under it. Silence, who had a hold on his ankle, followed.

Once inside, Nathan put the cup handle in his mouth, then knifed between a couple of big crates. Silence followed, still grasping his ankle. When he came to a barrel which had a stack of clothing piled atop it, he paused, reached back for Silence's hand and signaled her toward him. She came alongside him, pressed close to him. Again, Nathan took her hand and guided it to the barrel. Halfway up it, her hand touched a cork. Nathan dropped her hand, then felt for the cork with one hand and removed the cup handle from his mouth with the other. There was a sudden gurgle and a soft splashing, then quiet.

"Back out," Nathan whispered.

In minutes they were again seated on the tailgate of the Frane wagon, the cupful of whiskey and another cup of water between them.

"That was a handy cork," Silence said. "How'd you do it?"

"Borrowed an auger."

"I didn't know you liked to drink that much."

"I don't," Nathan said. "I let one barrel drain into the ground. Then I thought I'd save the other for trading purposes." He laughed. "An Indian selling a white man's whiskey to white men. I like that."

"Why do you hate Racklin so?"

"For roughing you up."

"I didn't know you knew he tried."

"Half the camp heard you cuss him out." He gestured toward the whiskey. "Well, there it is."

"Is there a trick to it?" Silence asked, picking up both cups and half raising them.

"Sure, with that stuff. Take a mouthful of water and don't swallow it. Then hold your breath, take a sip of whiskey, take another drink of water and swallow the works. Then let your breath out."

"That's so you won't taste it?"

"You'll taste it. That's so it won't make your throat bleed."

Silence's drink was not entirely successful; the last drink of water backed up a little and she coughed. However, Nathan saw by her grimace that she had caught the flavor of Racklin's forty rod, and he laughed silently.

When Silence had caught her breath, she said haltingly, "It tastes like the stuff we paint on a harness-galled horse."

Now Nathan took the cup of whiskey and drank a big swallow, putting out the fire with a cup of water. Immediately, he took another drink and he felt the raw stuff churn in his belly.

Watching, Silence said, "Please, don't do like those troopers did, Nathan."

"That's right, I've got no Lieutenant Milham to rescue me."

Silence suddenly gave a low laugh, remembering how she had slipped Milham's pistol away from him. Then her laugh ceased as she remembered him wrestling her. It was the first time a man had put his arms around her since she'd been grown and the experience was disturbing. He'd been immensely strong and his arm had almost cracked her rib cage as it mauled her breasts. He'd been rough and angry, perhaps rightly, she thought.

"Nathan, were you looking at the lieutenant when he came off his horse?"

"No, I was trying to break your arm." He looked at her. "Why?"

"I think he was mad."

"I looked at him later. Sure he was mad."

"Good."

Racklin's flare barely lighted the close half of Silence's face, but Nathan watched it as he asked, "Why do you hate him?"

Surprise came into her face. "Why? Don't you?"

"I feel sorry for him."

"Why?" Silence's anger almost made the word a curse.

"In the first place, you've made him look like a fool twice. In the second place, he's not the one to be mad at. Get mad at Congress. He's only working for them."

"He could have headed off that stampede from camp!" Silence said hotly.

"If his men had been mounted and if he knew that's what Hovey was going to do."

90

Silence considered this soberly. She and Nathan seldom disagreed, so his words troubled her. What Nathan had said in Milham's defense held a measure of truth, but still Milham represented naked force, something she disliked intensely. In the West she knew it was the accepted thing to openly despise the Army. During Indian troubles, the Army was always too late to avert disaster and usually too inept to catch and punish. It attracted the dregs of the Eastern cities and its officer corps was made up of men who had failed in civilian life. In what way was Milham different than other officers? He was handsome in a tin soldier fashion, but he was pompous and incompetent in spite of what Nathan said.

"You want any more of this whiskey?" Nathan asked.

Before Silence could answer, the distant voices of the Boomers were raised in a hymn, signaling the end of the meeting. Nathan pitched the whiskey out into the grass and rose, saying, "I'd better light the lantern."

He and Silence moved under the fly and while Nathan lighted the lantern and placed it on the repaired table, Silence stirred the fire. Boomer couples with their sleepy children passed by on their way to their wagons, bidding each other good night.

Presently Cap arrived and walking with him

was Catherine Henry. She nodded and smiled to Nathan and Silence and then said in a warm and throaty voice to Cap, "Thank you for your advice, Captain Frane. Good night, all."

When Catherine was gone, Silence asked, "What advice?"

"Oh, she's looking for something to do here." Cap's pretended indifference didn't fool Silence.

"Like sweet-talking older men?"

Cap gave her his regal stare. "Now what do you mean by that?"

"I notice whenever we hold a meeting, she's closest to you. What advice did you give her — to stand closer to you?"

In spite of his efforts to appear indifferent, Cap flushed. Then he said blandly, "Why it's a pleasure to talk with a handsome woman, but this was business. She wants to start up a school."

"Of what? Hunting men?" Silence knew she was getting fresh, but she could not stand the Henry woman with the bold and flirting ways that almost frightened these humble farmers. She was after a husband — any husband — and Cap conceivably was the head of her list.

"A plain school," Cap said shortly. "I told her the children were needed to help their parents this summer. When we have homes, it will be time enough for school."

He turned to Nathan. "Well, Nathan. Get paper and pen. I'm adding the news of Hovey's raid to the letter to Major Kelso."

"Where's Hovey live?" Nathan asked curiously.

"He said the first time he was here that his outfit was five miles east. Why?" Cap said.

"I just wanted to be sure and miss his place."

"You'll start early in the morning for Reno, Nathan." He looked at Silence. "Not a word from you about going with Nathan."

Silence nodded that she understood as Nathan headed for the wagon to get writing materials.

Silence asked then, "Are you going to tell the major that Milham's detail failed to protect us?"

Cap gave her a look of surprise. "Why most certainly. Why else would I be writing him?"

In his own tent, Lieutenant Milham was also writing, and to the same man. When he came to the account of the stampede through the camp, no matter how he phrased it, the words seemed to damn him for negligence. He had not been alert and Hovey had been daring, to sum it up. He refused to make excuses.

The Boomer camp wakened at first light and soon the breakfast fires had lifted a blanket of blue smoke over the whole camp. A distant rooster raucously greeted the day.

Nathan wolfed down his breakfast and was saddling his horse when Cap approached.

"Give me that letter to Major Kelso, Nathan. I've remembered something else."

Nathan was anxious to be off and he said, "Can't I tell him?"

"This must be a formal request for an Army doctor for Willie," Cap said stiffly, and held out his hand. Resignedly, Nathan searched in his saddle bag and pulled out Cap's letter. Cap took it and tramped back to the wagon and Nathan sighed. The formal request would turn into several pages, he knew. Cap would describe the accident and denounce both Hovey and the Army again before he made his request. *I'd be lucky to get away by noon,* Nathan thought.

It was only an hour and a half later when Cap rose from the table, handed the letter to Nathan and watched him mount and ride out.

Nathan crossed the creek. Reno was southwest; but he turned east. The sweet-smelling grass of the prairie was still heavy with yesterday's rain and the night's dew. *That's good,* Nathan thought.

His thoughts again returned to Hovey's stampede of yesterday and the resignation with which Cap and the other Boomers had accepted it. Before they went to sleep last night Cap, a little hurt that he and Silence had missed the council meeting, told of the decision arrived at. They would try to get seed and fence in Caldwell with some money down and, hopefully, generous credit. What were they going to do about Hovey? Nathan had asked. Whoever went to Caldwell would report the affair to the U. S. marshal, Cap had replied. The fact that there were nearly a hundred men, good people all, who had only a talking interest in wanting to punish Hovey puzzled Nathan. In school he had been drenched and inundated by the teachings of the Bible, but they had seemed thin things compared to the teachings of his father and his people. But apparently, the Boomers believed enough of the Bible to meekly turn the other cheek to Hovey. He didn't.

It was an hour after sunup when Nathan came to a small creek bordered by cottonwoods. Reasoning that Hovey's place was probably near water, Nathan climbed high in one of the cottonwoods and looked first downstream and then upstream. Far to the north he made out a couple of buildings in a clearing that bordered the stream.

Mounting again Nathan rode north and presently picked up a faint wagon track that barely showed through the tall prairie grass.

Where it came from Nathan couldn't guess, but he knew it went in the direction of the buildings he'd spotted.

Some time later he left the track and headed for a plum thicket. Then he tethered his horse and continued afoot, paralleling the track but keeping to cover. Presently he came to the building — a mean log shack and a sod-and-wood barn.

Nathan hunkered down behind a tree to watch. The corral was empty and no smoke issued from the chimney, and Nathan finally concluded there was no one inside. Boldly, then, he walked up to the shack, knocked, then, receiving no answer, entered.

He stepped into a large bunkroom and began his search. He supposed this place was Hovey's, but he had to make sure. But his search revealed no letters or clothing that gave a clue.

Leaving the shack, he went out to the barn. There, hanging on a nail, he found a branding iron. It was Diamond H, and Nathan remembered that Hovey's cattle had carried that brand.

Returning to the shack, Nathan started a fire in one of the bunks, using the grass-filled sacking mattress as a starter. Then, letting it burn, he took other mattresses to the barn, piled everything inflammable against the log part of the stable and touched a match to it.

Returning to the shack, he set a second fire in the kitchen, waited till it caught well, then went outside and headed back for his horse. Yesterday's rain, he knew, would prevent a prairie fire.

Some distance off he turned and saw the smoke rising. This wasn't much of a revenge, he knew, but it was the best he could do. At least it would let Hovey know that all the Boomers weren't sheep.

That same morning, Catherine Henry wakened at daylight in her bed behind the blanket partition in the Henry wagon. She could hear her brother, Ed, and his wife, Mary, in surly conversation as they went about preparing breakfast.

She should be helping, she knew, but she lay there a moment, remembering last night's meeting and her talk with Cap afterwards. Her conversation with Cap had been friendly and personal for the first time, and she knew he was attracted to her. She wondered, not for the first time, how much money Cap was worth. He had collected twenty-five dollars from each Boomer family for joining the Frane colony and he had organized other colonies before. Very likely he had a tidy sum in the bank in spite of his poormouthing.

He was older than she, of course, but that had its advantages in that he wouldn't live forever. True, if she married him, she would be married to a farmer like brother Ed. But was he a farmer, really? While he was building a sod house like the rest of the Boomers, he had broken no land. He *talked* land, rather than worked it. In essence, he lived by his wits, and wits were useful anywhere.

But there was Silence Frane to consider. Catherine knew that Silence bore no love for her. In that undeclared war between all women for the love (and the property, she added mentally) of a man she and Silence were natural enemies. The girl was sharp-tongued and callow, but bright. Still, rumor had it that Cap was still boss of his household and that was what counted.

Turning on her cot, she lifted the wagon canvas and peered out at the day which was cloudless after the rain. Bright as the day was, it would be another dreary one, she reflected as she dressed.

Stepping down from the tailgate step, she said good morning to her brother and Mary. Ed Henry was a burly man in his late thirties, as blond as Catherine was dark. His bib overalls and shirt were sun-bleached and the back of his plowman's neck was the color of mahogany. His broad face was cross and crafty, his good morning curt.

Mary, who was pregnant, handed Catherine her plate of food without speaking. There was a look of anguished martyrdom in her colorless face, as if announcing to the world that women were born to suffer and that she was suffering more than most.

Catherine said, "Ed, it's too wet to plow today, isn't it?"

"Why sure."

"Then can I ride Beau this morning if you won't be using him?"

Ed looked up. "But I will be using him. I'm taking the team to Fort Reno."

"Ed's crazy," Mary remarked to nobody in particular.

"Why are you going to Reno?"

"For wire, and to make a deal for my oats this fall."

Catherine felt a surge of excitement. "Oh, Ed, can I go along?"

Ed looked startled and put down his empty plate. "What for?"

Most of all to get away from here, Catherine thought. "Oh, Ed, there are so many things I need that you couldn't buy. Things for Mary, too. Besides I could cook and be company."

Ed looked at Mary and said, "I don't like leaving Mary alone."

"I'll make out," Mary said resignedly.

99

"Oh, Ed, there are a dozen neighbors within call. They'll do for Mary everything I could do. Besides, what could happen?" Catherine's tone had lost its pleading; it was abrupt, almost commanding, and Ed looked at her with surprise.

"It'll be a rough trip."

"Let it be," Catherine said curtly. "I'm not pregnant."

It took Trooper Harvey six days to make the round trip from the Boomer camp to Reno and back. The message he brought from Major Kelso curtly ordered Lieutenant Milham and his detail back to Reno.

When the detail had struck camp on this bland sunny morning, their activity had attracted the attention of the Boomers, so that as the detail rode past between the creek and the edge of camp, the Boomers had dropped their work and watched. Some of them had jeered and not a few of the children had run along-side the detail shrilling insults.

Lieutenant Milham, his back ramrod straight and eyes front, had spotted the Franes standing side by side watching the departure of the Army, and he had wondered if it wouldn't have been better to leave the bivouac in another direction, thus avoiding this further humiliation. Such action, however, would have implied that he and his detail were slinking away after some moral defeat. True, it was a temporary defeat, but he was not about to acknowledge it.

As the detail had pulled abreast the Franes, Cap Frane had raised his hand. Lieutenant Milham had signaled the detail to halt, and Cap and Silence had approached them.

"Leaving us, Lieutenant?" Cap had asked.

"Yes, Sir. Orders." Milham had not missed the faint smile that crossed Silence's face at his brief words.

"Does that mean you'll leave us alone?" Cap had asked.

Milham had nodded. "For now."

"But not for good?"

"I wouldn't judge so, but my new orders didn't mention it."

Silence had said then, "So the bullying isn't over?"

Milham had looked at her with irony. "No, but you can leave off being martyrs for a while now."

Silence had flushed. "You make that sound fairly ugly."

"I did at that."

Silence had said angrily, "When you come back, you'll find a town here."

Milham had nodded. "And I've already got

a name for it — Whine, Indian Territory."

He had turned, signaled his detail into motion, and rode on.

Now, a little less than an hour from Fort Reno, Lieutenant Milham rediscovered that he was grimly apprehensive of his reception by Major Kelso. His own account of the Hovey stampede and his part — or lack of part — in it had been sent ahead a day ago by courier. He was certain that Cap Frane had also sent an account to headquarters. This, added to his first dispatch reporting his inability to move the Boomers, was in sum an admission of possible negligence and certain incompetence. To top it off, he had four prisoner-troopers in his command who would go straight to the guardhouse for drunkenness, fighting and destruction of civilian property. *Quite an accomplishment on ten days' rations,* he thought sourly.

Not until they reached Darlington, the agency town across the river from Fort Reno, did Milham realize what day this was. The small settlement of the agency building, homes for employees, a couple of stores and a livery, seemed deserted. Ordinarily, it would be reasonably crowded with loafing Cheyenne and Arapaho and their families along with a scattering of the Indian police. This could only mean that today was the weekly beef issue to Indians, a day of tension for officers and troopers alike. Major Kelso would be harried and short of temper, Milham knew.

The detail crossed the river among the cottonwoods and entered the garrison grounds, heading for the stables. There, the detail took care of their mounts. Milham, however, did not unsaddle. When the men were finished, Milham told Corporal Byrd to assemble the detail, and when they were lined up, Milham spoke.

"Corporal, you will escort Troopers Ford, Bristol, Johnson, Ryan and Thompson to the guardhouse. They have been and are under arrest for drunkenness, fighting and destruction of civilian property. You may dismiss the rest of the detail."

Afterwards, Milham rode over to the headquarters building and learned from the duty sergeant that his hunch was correct: Major Kelso was at the beef issue at the corrals two miles west.

When Millham arrived at the beef issue, he reined in on the crest of land that sloped gently toward the far river. Nearest him were the onlookers — officers' wives and children, post loafers and visitors in a variety of vehicles. Beyond them was a half company of infantry, rifles stacked in a row, to the west of B Troop, consisting of a platoon of dismounted cavalry. Then came a vast open space of hoof-trampled meadow that stretched to the huge corral that was jammed with bawling beeves.

But the sight that always stirred Milham was the hundreds of Cheyenne and Arapaho Indians and their families scattered to the west of the big corral. They were seated on skins or blankets; standing in their blanket-wrapped buckskins and leaning on spears or rifles or mounted on their lean ponies. There were a hundred fires already kindled, and circulating among this vast army of Indians were the few blue-coated Indian police issuing to each Indian family the white slip of paper which entitled them to beef.

The issue day was always a tense one, Milham knew from experience. It was the day when the young bucks, forbidden to earn war honors, tried to prove themselves bold riders and good hunters. Deprived of the buffalo, they tried their hunting prowess on the cattle.

Even now, as one bawling steer was released from the corral chute at a bellowing run, a Cheyenne buck leaning over his pony's neck, took chase. Expertly, he hazed the running steer to the west, rode him down and then, riding close beside him, sank his spear into the steer's side. Sliding off his horse, he cut the steer's throat, then mounted and rode off.

His women and children ran out to the steer to butcher him, a chore beneath the brave's dignity. They would cook part of the steer immediately. There was the smell of blood everywhere, which seemed to excite man and beast. This parody of hunting seemed to inflame the Indians, reminding them of a hunting and warlike past before the white man came and moved them from their old hunting grounds to this alien reservation. The whole garrison knew that some foolhardy act on the part of either soldiers or Indians could erupt into a spontaneous battle between the two forces. The Indians greatly outnumbered the undermanned garrison, and it was a miracle that they had not yet taken advantage of this to attempt an uprising.

Milham put his horse down the slope and soon saw Major Kelso talking with Lieutenant Evans behind the dismounted troopers. They were standing in conversation, holding the reins of their mounts. When Milham swung off his horse and saluted, Major Kelso said drily, "Well, you got back on barbecue day, Scott. How are your Boomers?"

"Still there, Sir, but I don't claim them."

Both Kelso and Evans laughed and now Major Kelso said, "Let's sit down over there," gesturing loosely to a spot out of earshot of the lounging troopers. Both men moved off and Kelso chose the place and sank down on the grass. Milham sat down beside him, took off his hat and placed it on the grass.

"How's the hurt boy?" Kelso asked.

Milham looked at him blankly. "Sir?"

"The Boomer lad with the broken leg."

"I didn't know there was one, Sir."

Major Kelso's broad face held a look almost of disbelief. "Why, Frane sent a message by an Indian asking for a doctor. Didn't you meet Doc Cummings on the way?"

"There was no road till we hit the cattle trail, Sir. No, we didn't see him." Milham could feel blood flushing into his face.

"And you didn't know about the Boomer lad? Strange." Kelso's voice held wonder rather than censure. "Didn't you talk with the Boomers?"

"Just after the stampede, Sir. Maybe they didn't know about the boy then. When we left, I talked with Frane. He didn't mention it."

This, Milham knew, sounded like an excuse and he was furious with himself and appalled at his ignorance. He had to come back to Reno to find out what had happened at the Boomer camp. But he continued stubbornly.

"You see, Sir, after that drunken brawl, I put the camp off limits. Then, after the stam-

106

pede, the Boomers were so angry with us, they wouldn't come over. Not even the children."

"There was no communication between you?"

"None, Sir."

To confess this was the final ignominy, yet his conduct at the time had seemed reasonable to him. Yet he continued doggedly.

"Sir, if I explain the situation there, it will sound as if I'm excusing myself."

"Not to me, go ahead."

Milham took a deep breath and plunged. "All the time we were there, Sir, there wasn't a civil word exchanged between us and the Boomers. From the beginning we were treated like foreign troops on their native soil. Even the site of our bivouac was claimed by one of them."

"You didn't mention that in your report."

"It wasn't important. The only reason I mention it now is to point out their hostility. That brawl by the Frane wagon worsened things. The stampede finished it."

Kelso asked curiously, "Could you have stopped the stampede?"

Milham's brow furrowed in thought. He wanted to be very sure about what he said next. "At first I had no reason to. It was pretty obvious that Hovey was trying to destroy their crops. It didn't seem to me to be any of the Army's business, since both Hovey and the Boomers were in the wrong." Still frowning, Milham absently raised his hand and scratched his mustache with projecting thumb. "Even when the cattle headed for camp I thought the fifty or so Boomers afoot and the dozen mounted men could turn them. When I saw they couldn't, it was too late for us to help."

Kelso grunted and Milham could not interpret it.

"I'm afraid I handled things badly, Sir."

Kelso looked at him sharply, then smiled faintly. "Yes, you probably did, but there are some situations that simply can't be handled well. They don't allow of any solution." He paused, then said wryly, "The Department of the Missouri orders the Boomers pushed back without the use of violence. The Boomers won't move even when we call in enough troops to move them. Any solution? You think I'm handling this well? You think the Department is?"

Milham thanked him silently, but it did not ease his feeling that he had botched a job.

"Tell me," Kelso said abruptly, "how did that Frane girl — what's her name, Surprise?"

"Silence." At the major's look of surprise, Milham added, "That wasn't a command, Sir,

Silence is her name."

The major smiled and nodded and then said abruptly, "How did she get your pistol?"

"Lifted it when I was looking the other way."

Now the major rose, and Milham picked up his hat and rose also.

"That's the only thing in your report that made embarrassing reading, Scott. That's all, and thank you."

Jess Hovey had left the herd with orders to his hands to trail his steers slowly toward Reno, allowing them to graze often. The steers weren't due until next week and Hovey hoped to put back some of the tallow they had run off in the stampede.

Hovey rode on into Reno with nothing much on his mind, but a deep satisfaction within him. His stampede had come off successfully and the Boomers' crops had largely been destroyed. Would it move them? If it didn't, he'd do it again and again.

Meanwhile, with his crew and cook on the trail, he could play some poker, drink a little and see if he couldn't pick up some horses at Reno.

The night of the day of the beef issue found him in Edmond's next to the officers' bar. It was thronged with off-duty troopers, cowhands from lease outfits and transient riders.

As Hovey mounted the steps of the veranda, he had seen the distant myriad campfires of Indians whose tepees clustered around the outskirts of Darlington across the river, and he knew they would be feasting tonight.

Inside, the smoke of the barroom trailed a blue banner over the heads of the drinkers and gamblers. The gaming tables were not nearly so crowded as the bar, since most troopers had barely enough money to drink, let alone gamble.

Hovey bought a bottle and a fistful of cigars, then took a chair at an empty gambling table.

Pouring a drink, he downed it, then lighted a cigar and looked about the room. He knew a few of the riders for leasees, but there was none he wanted to talk with.

He was pouring a second drink when he felt a hand on his shoulder and looked up to regard the smiling face of a big man of fifty, dressed in a dark townsman's suit.

Hovey smiled and put out his hand, but did not rise. "Why, Brady, you son of a gun. What are you doing up here?"

They shook hands as Brady said, "Been to Caldwell fightin' with commission houses."

"You got a herd on the way up? Sit down."

Brady pulled out a chair while Hovey rose and procured another glass from the bar. Returning, he put glass and bottle before Brady and was slacking into his chair when Brady said, "Reckon you ran into some bad luck, Jess."

Hovey frowned and finished seating himself. "First I heard of it."

"I stopped by your place."

"Nobody there."

Brady looked at him sharply, "Hell, the place ain't there. It burned down. Didn't you know it?"

Hovey regarded him carefully to see if this was some practical joke. Then he said, "It was there a week ago."

"It's level now, believe me."

"Lightning?"

"Don't reckon lightning could hit the cabin *and* the barn."

Hovey sat motionless, scowling at his glass, mentally assessing the loss. Everything he owned that wasn't on his back — save horses and cattle — was in that shack. It wasn't much, but it was all. A slow wrath came to Hovey then. He'd made a fire the morning he left and conceivably it could have fired the shack. But not the barn. No, this fire had been set — and he thought he knew who did it. It had to be the Boomers, paying him back for destroying their crops. The Indians never bothered him and he'd always made trail hands welcome. No, it *had* to be the Boomers.

"Did it fire the grass?" Hovey asked.

When Brady said no, Hovey breathed an inaudible sigh of relief. A really good grass fire could wipe out his herd. Thinking back now, Hovey judged that the fire had been set shortly after the last rain which was the day of the stampede. Otherwise, the prairie would have caught.

Brady had a drink and a cigar while they discussed the prospect of the coming market, but Hovey's heart wasn't in it. When he could decently leave, he rose, shook Brady's hand and stepped out onto the long veranda. Tramping down it, he found a secluded chair and slacked into it.

The whiskey he had drunk, instead of exhilarating him, sat sourly on his stomach, and he knew it was because of his anger. The Boomers apparently intended to fight and he was not the man to refuse them. His boyhood had been spent in the Comanche country where burnings and pillage had been common. When a man returned to his home and found it burned to the ground, with perhaps his family in it, he buried his dead, gathered his kin and friends and hunted down the Comanches responsible. Retaliation, then, was a part of him, but how to effect it was another matter.

More stampeding cattle? The Boomers were not likely to be caught off guard again and

112

they would slaughter his beef. Go to the Army with his protest? That was useless, since they had refused help all along. Gun down Cap Frane? That wouldn't be hard, but what would it accomplish? The Boomers had their land now and didn't need Cap. They would bury him and stay right there.

No, Hovey thought, he needed Cap alive because only Cap had the influence to lead the Boomers off his grass.

Was Cap bribable? Hovey doubted it and besides he didn't have bribe money. Then what else could change Cap's mind?

Suddenly, a thought came to Hovey with an abruptness that made him sit up straight in his chair.

Next morning after breakfast Hovey stopped by Edmond's bar for an after-breakfast drink, then stepped out on the long veranda and turned left, heading for the livery up the street. The street was busy with wagon traffic and the tie rail in front of Edmond's store held teams and wagons and saddle horses. Even this early, loafers were occupying the veranda chairs.

Ahead of him, sitting by herself, Hovey saw a dark-haired woman. As he passed her, glancing sidelong, he had a vague impression that he'd seen her before, but he couldn't place her immediately. He was ten paces past her when it came to him. Halting abruptly, he searched his memory. This Boomer girl's name was Henry — Caroline? No, Catherine. She had wanted a cook job.

Now he turned and tramped back and halted in front of her. Removing his hat he said, "Good morning, Miss Henry."

Catherine looked at him carefully, her eyes faintly hostile. "You seem to know me, but I don't know you."

"You asked me for a cook's job."

Catherine nodded and smiled faintly. "I remember now. Does anyone want a cook?"

"Nobody that I've asked," Hovey said easily. He sank into a barrel chair next to hers and continued. "What brings you to Reno?"

"I came with my brother. He's buying supplies."

Her friendliness indicated to Hovey that she did not know his name, and he wondered if it would make any difference if she did. He decided to find out.

"My name's Jess Hovey, Miss Henry. Mean anything to you?"

Catherine appraised him and her eyes held no rancor. "Those were your cattle, then."

"They were mine."

"They broke a boy's leg."

Hovey looked troubled and told the truth. "I didn't know that. Still, it's lucky some of

114

your people and my men weren't trampled."

Catherine nodded almost indifferently, and Hovey could see no anger in her. Encouraged, he went on. "How are your sodbuster friends?"

"They're no friends of mine, but your stampede is costing us all fence money."

"You, too?"

Catherine looked at him with something close to amusement. "I have twenty dollars to my name. No, eighteen after this morning."

"Want some?" Hovey asked bluntly and hastened to add, "To take it won't shame you."

"Why would you give me money?" Catherine seemed more interested than insulted.

"For a simple favor you can do me."

"I'm flattered, but what's the favor?"

Hovey rubbed a hand over the remaining close-cropped hair of his balding head. He was so unaccustomed to having his hat off in the daytime that he felt naked.

Here was his chance, and it had been handed to him on a silver platter if he played it right, he thought now.

"Miss Henry, didn't I see a tent saloon in the Boomer camp when I talked with Frane?"

"Yes, there's one. Will Racklin runs it."

"What sort of man is he?"

"What's any saloonkeeper?"

Hovey smiled thinly because he had anticipated an answer of this sort. "You know him?"

"We say hello. Why?"

Hovey shifted in his chair and put his elbows on his knees, reviewing what he was about to say, and it seemed plausible.

"Miss Henry, one of my hands got in a shootin' scrape with a soldier, a bad one. The Army is lookin' for him and so's a U. S. marshal. He needs a place to hide."

"Isn't there an awful lot of country to get lost in here?" Catherine asked dryly.

"No, ma'am. Not with the Indian police and the Indians lookin' for you. But them and the Army would never think of your Boomer camp. If this Racklin would hide him until I can get things quieted down, I'd pay him for it."

Catherine frowned. "Why don't you ask Racklin?"

Hovey looked at her with feigned astonishment. "Me ride into your Boomer camp after what my cattle done? I don't reckon I'd last five minutes, would I? Even a girl took a shot at me."

Catherine nodded slowly. "You want me to ask Racklin if he'd hide out your man, is that it?"

"Yes, without naming me. Make up a name, because if you named me, he'd turn it down."

116

Catherine considered. This seemed a harmless enough favor. It wouldn't be she who was hiding a fugitive. It amounted only to asking Racklin a question, getting his answer and relaying it to Hovey. This Hovey was a clever man, she couldn't help thinking, for it was absolutely true that neither the marshal, the Indian police nor the Army would think of the camp as a hiding place.

"Is your man dangerous?" Catherine asked.

"He's worked for me for years," Hovey lied quietly. "Fact is, three drunken soldiers tried to take his Indian girl away from him and" — he searched for the right word — "harm her. He shot one of the soldiers. They all lied to their commanding officer. The girl was hurt in the scuffle and that brought in the Indian police."

Hovey, watching her face, saw outrage and sympathy there. She had no way of checking on his fabricated story and wouldn't bother to anyway, he was sure.

"All right, Mr. Hovey. I'll talk with Racklin."

Hovey reached in his pocket and pulled out a handful of double eagles. He took out two and extended them to Catherine.

"One is for your trouble and I thank you. The other is for Racklin to bind the bargain, with more to come."

Catherine hesitatingly accepted them. "It's

117

too much," she said quietly.

"No. I'd have to pay a man to ride to your camp and talk with Racklin. You'll be doing what he would do. Oh, now that I think of it, I'll have to be in touch with my man if Racklin hides him. How do you folks get your mail?"

"It's dropped off at the Pond Creek stage station. Once a week somebody rides over and picks it up."

Hovey nodded and rose. "Good. Now, do you remember where you met me? I'll be there in the brush after supper a week from today. Is that all right?"

"A week from today," Catherine repeated and then added shyly, "You're very generous, Mr. Hovey."

Hovey put on his hat and then touched its brim with a gesture of courtesy.

"And you're very accommodating, Miss Henry. Good-by."

☆4☆

A week later, Hovey was squatting in the brush alongside Big Piney Creek observing the Boomer camp in the settling evening. He noticed with bitterness that since he'd seen it last, more buildings had started and some homes were nearing completion. Even some of the fields were partially fenced with barbed wire. A new building had risen past the bend in the creek to the south.

He watched the Boomers coming and going among the wagons and buildings and, presently, a figure separated from them and came in his direction. It was Catherine Henry and as she came closer, strolling idly, he saw she had thrown a shawl over her shoulders as if she were setting out on a solitary walk.

Hovey rose at her approach but did not leave his hiding place. When she was close, Catherine Henry saw him and then halted.

"Good evening, Miss Henry."

"You have a good memory, Mr. Hovey." She paused. "Will Racklin will hide your man for twenty dollars a week."

Hovey smiled grimly. "I could send him to

119

New York for that."

"Shall I tell him no, then?"

Hovey shook his head in negation. "There's no time for bargaining. I accept. Tell him my man will come in tonight after the camp's asleep. He understands about keeping this quiet, doesn't he?"

Catherine nodded. "He asked me if there was a reward posted for your man."

I'll bet he did, Hovey thought, but he said, "The way I get it, the Army only offers a reward for the return of deserters. They can't offer a reward for the return of a civilian unless he works for them."

"I'll tell him," Catherine said.

"Don't bother, Miss Henry. My man will tell him himself."

"I must go or they'll be looking for me."

Hovey nodded. "Thank you again, Miss Henry. You've helped a good man."

He observed her flush of pleasure at his words. He stood motionless a moment watching her start back toward the camp. She was a handsome woman, he thought, and in other circumstances he would have called on her and courted her. Right now, however, there was no room for a woman in his life. Turning, he crossed the narrow creek in the dusk and tramped back to a cottonwood motte where his horse was tied alongside a second saddled horse. Stepping into the saddle, he headed upstream, leading the second horse.

A half mile to the north, he came to a small feeder creek to the Big Piney which bisected a lush meadow. Here he unsaddled both horses, cached the saddles in the limbs of a nearby tree, then staked out both horses, placing the picket pins near enough to the stream so that the horses could reach water. When he was finished, it was dark.

Afterward, he headed back toward the Boomer camp, using the silhouettes of the stream bottom trees as guides. The Boomer camp, he was reasonably certain, would soon be asleep, like any other community of farmers who had no other use for night.

Approaching the camp, he saw that the supper fires had been extinguished and that only a few of the wagons showed a light behind their canvas; a few of the camp dogs were barking as their owners cursed them to silence.

Hovey circled the camp and picked up the light from Will Racklin's kerosene flare. Halting, he sat down on the ground, crossing his legs, and fashioned a cigarette by feel. He had finished it and had a match in his hand when he suddenly remembered that the flare of a match might give away his presence. Swearing mildly, he tossed away the cigarette and then summoned up patience.

It was half an hour before the last lamp in the wagons was extinguished. Racklin's tent flare had been doused, too, but a faint glow of light behind the canvas told Hovey that Racklin was waiting.

Hovey rose and moved toward Racklin's tent. When he reached its side wall, he halted and looked up the street which had once been grassy but was now trampled and rutted. Even in the darkness his keen eyes could pick out the big Frane wagon with its extended fly. There, he thought bitterly, Cap Frane would be sleeping and Hovey was willing to bet that even in sleep his face would hold the same self-righteousness that it held in all his waking hours.

Hovey swung under the plank bar, pulled aside the tent flap and stepped into the tent. Only after he closed the flap did he turn and look about him.

Will Racklin sat in his barrel chair alongside a crate which held a lamp that was turned low. The forepart of his tent held a small stove, a table and two cots end to end that marked the dividing line between his stacked trade goods and his living quarters. Each man looked at the other in deliberate appraisal. Hovey was looking at a soft blob of a man whose lethargy seemed monumental; Racklin was looking at a saddle-leaned man with the palest, meanest eyes he had ever seen.

Hovey spoke first. "Name's Carter."

Racklin nodded and neither man offered to shake hands. Racklin was curious but he could think of no way to begin a conversation that would ease his curiosity. It was like trying to think of small talk while you were looking down a pair of gun barrels.

After briefly examining the tent, Hovey said, "You got blankets?"

"All you want to buy."

Racklin's voice, Hovey decided, was the only firm thing about him. It was loud with a false heartiness.

Hovey asked quietly, "You talk to yourself much?"

Racklin looked puzzled, then smiled faintly. "No, I got damn little to say to myself."

"Anybody close by would think you're talking to me or to yourself. Pretty soon they'll wonder who you got in here."

Again puzzlement came into Racklin's wide face. "You mean you aren't going to let anybody know you're here."

"No. Neither are you."

"You mean you're going to stay in this tent all day?"

Hovey nodded. "I'll move around at night."

123

Anger crossed Racklin's face and vanished. "I didn't figure having you underfoot all the time."

"Figure on it now." Hovey's tone of voice was cold and blunt and somehow his words were contrived to be an order.

Hovey took one step deeper into the tent, placed hands on hips, but his glance had never left Racklin's face. "My friend, let's settle one thing: there's no reward money on me. I don't reckon there would be reward money on me if I killed you." He paused, isolating what was to come next. "Think about it."

The protest and outrage that showed in Racklin's face never found voice. He said, almost gently, "Yes, *Sir*."

Hovey spent the next morning flat on his belly in the back half of the tent. He had propped up the canvas of the tent's side wall a few inches so that he could observe the comings and goings around the Frane wagon down the way. Racklin's customers, mostly women and children, drifted in and out of the tent, but Hovey, well hidden, ignored them.

At midmorning, three wagons minus their canvas and each pulled by two teams, pulled into camp and then halted by the Frane wagon. Hovey watched the short conversation between the lead teamster and Silence, after which Silence headed for the creek. In a matter of minutes, she returned with Cap Frane, who climbed into his wagon and returned with a sheet of paper.

Hovey saw that the principal freight in the three wagons were fence posts and rows of barbed wire. It was easy to guess that the rest of the load was mainly seed for crops. After consulting Cap's sheet of paper, the lead teamster beckoned the other two teamsters and showed them the paper. Afterward the wagons split up and Hovey lost interest. Cap Frane disappeared and Silence, apparently finished with her early morning chores, climbed into the wagon and moments later reappeared, sat on the bench under the fly and opened a book. Several women accompanied by children carrying bundles of laundry passed down the rough street, apparently headed for the creek. Then for several long minutes the camp was quiet, seemingly abandoned in the lull of a hot spring morning that smelled faintly of dust.

Hovey could make nothing of this much of Silence's day. He had watched her cook breakfast, prepare other food, go for her father and then sit down with a book. Was this the normal pattern of her day? Didn't she walk, visit, do the family laundry, or ride, he wondered, knowing that in half a morning, he could not begin to understand the pattern of her day.

His speculation was interrupted by Racklin's brassy greeting to a man named Barney. It was followed by small talk that Hovey couldn't hear and then Racklin and presumably Barney entered the tent.

"Let's put it down here," Racklin said. "I've got to sort the stuff."

They left the tent, returned again, left once more and came back with the final load. Hovey presumed this was freight for Racklin's store.

Now whistling thinly, Racklin busied himself at unpacking the freight and Hovey, with the hot sun on the tent, put his head on his forearm and drowsed. He did not hear Racklin leave the tent.

With two new bolts of material under his arm, Racklin ducked under the plank bar and headed toward the Frane wagon. At his approach, Silence looked up from her book and then back to her book. She heard Racklin halt.

"I've got some new dress material come in. I wanted to give you first chance at it."

Silence turned the page. Slowly lifting her glance, she saw that Racklin had leaned a bolt of material against his leg and had partly unrolled a second bolt of material, blue in color, and was holding it under his chin. The material was touching his boot tops.

"Like it?" Racklin asked.

Silence said sweetly, "It's not your color, honey."

Racklin flushed and said angrily, "I was only trying to do you a favor."

"You can. Go away."

"Don't you want to see the other material?"

"Aren't I looking at it? I don't recommend it for you, either."

Racklin rolled up the material as Silence returned to her book.

"You had your chance. Now I'm going to show them to Catherine Henry."

"Why her?"

"Because she's the next handsomest woman in camp."

"Don't you think those colors are a little young for her?"

There was a tartness in Silence's tone of voice that did not escape Racklin, and it angered him so that he immediately voiced his thoughts.

"What the hell's bitin' you, Silence?"

"Not you, but you try."

"What's the matter with Catherine Henry?"

"Nothing, if she lived in San Francisco."

Racklin made a loose gesture with spread hands. "Nothing I can say or do pleases you. I bring over something I think you'll like and you — you spit on it."

"Why come, then?"

Racklin's hands fell in an eloquent gesture of hopelessness. "I quit."

"I don't believe that. You'll never quit."

It took Racklin a moment to backtrack on what he had last said. "All right, why should I quit? You're a pretty girl."

Silence looked up. "Will you marry me, Sir?" she asked archly.

"I don't have to marry a girl just because she's pretty."

"That's for damn sure." She paused. "You think Catherine is pretty?" At Racklin's nod, she asked, "Isn't she nice spoken? Isn't she better spoken than I am?"

Racklin said nothing. Silence continued, "Why don't you marry her?"

Racklin's eyes widened a little. "She wouldn't have me."

"Tell me why she wouldn't."

Racklin mused a moment and then said, "I sell whiskey."

"She drinks it, too."

"She does not," Racklin answered heatedly.

"Then why has she stopped at your tent a half dozen times in the last week?"

"I sell lots else besides whiskey. Like dress goods."

"Her eyesight must be very good if she can look across the bar into a dark tent and see

128

what you're selling."

"Why do you care who I talk to?" Racklin demanded.

"I don't, as long as it isn't me." She put her book down and rose. "I spend five minutes a day trying to think of something funny. Your time's up, Mr. Racklin." She pushed past him and entered the wagon and Racklin, a bolt of goods under each arm, headed back for his tent.

When Racklin stepped into the tent, he found Hovey among the trade goods waiting for him.

"Who's the girl?" Hovey asked, although he knew.

"Silence Frane, Cap's girl."

"See much of her?"

Racklin grunted in disgust. "All she'll let me, and that's not at all."

"You mean you don't go walkin' with her?"

"That's what I mean."

Hovey frowned. "Well, doesn't somebody?"

Racklin regarded him with curiosity. "There's a young Injun works for Cap. He's around her a lot, but nobody else."

"What's the matter with the men in this camp?"

"It ain't the men. It's her."

"Don't she ever ride?"

"Not that I know of." Racklin observed him closely. "You seem kind of interested, Carter."

Hovey shook his head. "Not in her especially. I just can't figure out this camp. You don't court a girl with neighbors so close they could swish flies off your neck. And the girls won't walk out."

"Some will."

"But not her." Hovey shook his head in disbelief. "What does she do? Live all the time in that wagon?"

Of all the people in camp, Racklin was in the best position to report on Silence's day, since she was in his sight most of the day.

"Just about. She visits some during the day. Since they put up the bath house, she goes down there almost every night after supper."

"Bath house?"

Racklin nodded. "By the creek. The women made the men put it up. It's pretty far to lug water up to here. Besides, I reckon they were afraid of being caught in the bare."

The bath house must be the new building he'd noticed, Hovey thought. Well, he had the information he wanted and if Racklin was curious, let him be.

Hovey spent the remainder of the day alternately dozing and planning. After their wretched supper of sour-dough pancakes and dried peaches, he resumed his surveillance of the Frane wagon. He had noted last night that in order to use all the daylight hours, the men worked late which, in turn, put supper late.

Cap Frane and the Indian arrived at the wagon just at dusk and they ate under the fly by lantern light. Before they had finished, Racklin lighted the kerosene flare and took his seat behind the plank bar ready for the evening's visits. Hovey watched while Silence washed the dishes and the Indian dried them. Afterwards, Silence disappeared into the wagon while Frane and the Indian brought out a checkerboard and began to play. Presently, Silence came out of the wagon with a towel draped around her neck, and a lighted kerosene lamp in her hand. She exchanged the lamp for the lantern, watched the game a moment and then walked out into the night in the direction of the creek.

Hovey lifted up the rear canvas of the tent, rolled under it, came to his feet and, avoiding the lighted wagons, began his circle of the camp at an awkward run that was hindered by his high-heeled cowman's boots.

Clear of the camp, he immediately picked up the distant figure of Silence illuminated by the lantern. Wherever the bath house was, Hovey thought, it was unlighted, which meant that Silence for the next few minutes would be alone.

Walking toward her, hidden by the night, Hovey presently saw the frame building loom up in the circle of light cast by Silence's lantern. She rounded the corner of the building and the light disappeared. Now Hovey hurried his pace and saw a dim light appear behind a curtained window.

Moving up to the side of the building, Hovey saw that it was doorless and he assumed that the entrance would be on the side nearest the creek. Silently rounding the corner, he saw the oblong of light whose further tip touched the creek. Then came the sound of a stove's fire being stirred with a poker and then abruptly a shadow was cast in the oblong of light. By that time Hovey was flattened against the building by the door, his gun drawn.

The shadow loomed larger and then Silence, a bucket in her hand, stepped into the doorway. Swiftly, Hovey raised his gun and Silence, attracted by the whisper of cloth rubbing against cloth, started to turn her head in the direction from which the sound came.

Hovey brought down the gun barrel smartly across Silence's head. Without uttering so much as a whisper, Silence's knees folded and she pitched forward, the bucket dropping from her hand. Hovey lunged for her and caught her in midfall. Holstering his gun, he knelt, lifted Silence to his shoulder, kicked the bucket into the stream and then vanished with her into the night.

It was Nathan who wakened first just before false dawn. Rolling out of his blankets laid out beside the sleeping Cap, he listened a moment for any movement behind the canvas partition which would tell him that Silence was awake. Hearing nothing, he stepped out of the wagon, lighted the lamp which was still on the table and set about building a fire in the small iron stove. The racket he made usually wakened Silence and Cap if they were still sleeping.

His morning chores after building the fire were simple enough. From the water barrel ironed to the side of the wagon, he dipped out enough water to fill the tea kettle, which he placed on the stove. Afterwards, he took out tin cups, granite plates, tin knives and forks and set the table. Following that, he went over to the brush corral which held their five horses, drove them down to water at the creek, then staked them out on fresh grass.

Looking around him now, he saw that the lantern was missing from its nail on the wagon side, and he wondered crossly what Silence had done with it. Then it occurred to him that it really didn't matter since it was getting light anyway.

By the time Nathan had staked out the horses, it was full day and the camp was astir. As he approached the wagon, he saw Cap standing under the fly, hands on hips. He was alone, which was strange, Nathan thought. As Nathan stepped under the fly, Cap saw him.

"Where's Silence?" Cap asked.

"Still asleep?"

"She's not asleep. She's not even here. Her blankets weren't slept in."

Cap and Nathan regarded each other soberly and silently. It was pointless for either of them to suggest that Silence might have stayed with a friend since Boomer wagons were far too crowded to sleep guests.

The lantern, Nathan thought, and he was already in motion.

"Where're you going?" Cap asked.

"To the bath house."

Cap fell in beside him, and they both headed toward the creek. Impatiently, Nathan broke into a run, leaving Cap behind. As he rounded the corner of the bath house closest to the creek, the first thing he saw was the half-submerged bucket which Hovey had kicked into the creek. Moving carefully on moccasined feet, Nathan approached the door frame and at one swift glance saw that the door was open and the lantern placed on a bench, still burning. By that time Cap, breathing heavily, rounded the corner, and without turning, Nathan held out his arm to bar the way.

"The lantern's still burning," Nathan said. Then he squatted down on his haunches and regarded the scuffed ground in front of the door. The grass on the short path to the creek had been worn away and in the dirt were the prints of the shoes of many women. Close to the door, however, was a set of different prints. They were a man's, Nathan noted. The man had worn cowman's narrow-heeled, pointed boots. The morning dew still held on the path which argued that the prints had been made in the night. Carefully, Nathan followed them to the creek where they entered the water.

When Nathan stepped into the water, Cap asked, "Where are you going?"

Nathan didn't answer as he waded the shallow stream and emerged on the far bank. A few minutes search verified what he had already guessed. The owner of the boots, once in the stream, had kept to it.

Nathan recrossed the stream to Cap and he felt almost unable to believe what the tracks had told him.

"What?" Cap demanded.

Before answering, Nathan, avoiding the path, looked at the ground beside the door. Again, there were the familiar prints. Now Nathan looked up at Cap and flattened himself against the wall.

"A man wearing cowman's boots stood here after Silence had left the lantern on the bench. She picked up the bucket and stepped out the door. He picked her up, carried her to the creek and walked up or down it with her," Nathan said emotionlessly.

"How do you know he picked her up?" Cap asked in frightened disbelief.

Taking a step, Nathan again hunkered down by the tracks and pointed. "This boot heel closest to the door is shallow. This boot heel deepens all the way to the creek."

"But who would want to take Silence, and what for? What for?" Cap asked in anguish.

An almost overwhelming grief engulfed Nathan, and for a moment, he could not talk. And with his grief was mingled both shame and anger. Cap had asked a question that he would not be proud to answer, but one that he must.

"Hovey took her, Cap."

Cap looked at him searchingly before he said, "You're guessing."

"But guessing right." Nathan paused, for

136

this was hard to get out. To look in his eye now was almost impossible, but he made his glance meet Cap's. "You see, I burned Hovey's shack and barn to the ground. That was to pay him back for the stampede. Now he's paying you back for what I did, Cap."

"I see," Cap said. There was no reproof in his voice, only sorrow. For many moments he stood lost in thought, and then he asked, "What will Hovey do with her? He has no place to keep her."

Nathan said quietly, "She's a woman and she's beautiful, Cap."

New shock came into Cap's face. "No," he said flatly.

Should he tell Cap the rest of it? No, Cap had had enough. If he pointed out to Cap that the tracks showed no sign of struggle from Silence, which argued that Hovey knocked her unconscious, Cap would go out of his mind.

"Are you suggesting rape, Nathan?"

Nathan only nodded once. *If it's happened, I'll kill myself,* Nathan thought.

A great shuddering sigh came from Cap. "I can't believe it. I *won't* believe it, Nathan. You understand, I *won't.*"

Nathan said nothing, waiting for Cap's inevitable question, and when it came, Nathan had the answer.

"What do we do, Nathan?"

"He would take her far enough away from camp so that her screams wouldn't be heard. Why don't we turn out our people on a search?"

Cap was now staring at the ground. He neither moved nor spoke for so long that Nathan touched his arm.

"Did you hear me, Cap?"

"I heard you," Cap said quietly. "Yes. A search." He turned and now they both hurried back to the waking camp. Immediately after reaching the wagon, Cap picked up the stove poker, moved over to the triangle used to call council meetings and beat it furiously.

Immediately the Boomer families left their breakfast fires and hurried to the clearing in front of the Frane wagon. As they assembled, the rumors started. There was a grass fire on the prairie that threatened them. What else would call for a meeting at this hour? Another rumor had it that a company of troopers was on its way.

When the Boomers were all assembled, Cap raised both hands, and the talk dribbled off into silence.

"My friends, my daughter Silence was forcibly taken from this camp last night. We think our enemy Hovey took her."

He went on to explain the evidence shown

138

on the path from the bath house to the creek, and then he paused, letting this shocking news sink in. There was an immediate swell of voices and Cap let the talk run on for a minute, then raised his arms again.

When he had their attention, he continued. "Silence may be lying hurt out on the prairie where the brute abandoned her. Or she may have been taken far away. All we can do now is to search the surrounding prairie and timber."

Here Cap's voice broke and tears that he did not attempt to hide ran down his ruddy, furrowed face. Some of the more emotional women with no special affection for Silence but with deep sympathy for her plight began to weep softly.

Again Cap gestured for silence. When he was given it, he said, "Many of you have never been out of camp, and it is easy to get lost in the ocean of grass around us. Form a line to the west and keep each other in sight. When the line is formed, we will begin a swing to the south. Those of you who have horses can ride at the outer edge of the circle. Take food and water with you and be sure to return by nightfall." His glance moved to take in the whole assemblage. "I hope you will understand that I am not ordering you to search for Silence. I am begging you to help."

By the time the Boomers had scattered with instructions to form their line to the west, Nathan had three horses saddled and was waiting at the brush corral. The women and children who had no mounts started filing past him. In the chill of morning sunlight, the first of them began to line out and hold, waiting for the rest to pass them and take up stations. The mounted men with some women headed past them, riding to the west.

Presently Cap approached the corral, and in the sharp sunlight, his face looked ravaged. He paid no heed to the expressions of sympathy that were extended to him by the passing people. Hauling up by Nathan, he accepted the reins Nathan extended to him, and they both mounted in silence.

The next hours were the purest hell for Nathan. He was waiting for a cry which would be passed down the line that Silence had been found. Hour after hour as the search continued Nathan's dismal feeling of guilt increased. He alone was responsible for what had happened to Silence. If he had wanted to avenge the stampede, why hadn't he done it personally and openly instead of anonymously? His act had been blamed on the Boomers generally, and Hovey had retaliated against the Boomers' leader in the cruelest way he knew. If Silence were found, Nathan knew, he would ride out,

leaving the Franes and his beloved Silence forever, for he could never summon the courage
to face her.

It was midafternoon when the farthest rider
signaled to the next rider, who in turn beckoned to Nathan. The message died with Nathan. *Now's the time to go, to simply ride out
of the country.* No, he could not leave until he
knew what had happened to Silence. He didn't
have to talk to her, but he did have to know
that she was alive and in safe hands.

He turned his horse and lifted him into a
gallop, following the rider who had beckoned.
When he arrived at the spot where the two
riders were halted and dismounted, he saw
they were talking, and a vast relief flooded
him. They would not be talking if Silence
were there. When Nathan reined in by the
two men, his glance took in the scene. Horses
had been staked out in a small meadow. He
saw where grass was cropped and there were
fresh droppings. Nathan swung down as one
of the men said, "There's been horses here,
but no signs of a camp."

Nathan didn't answer. He made a slow circle of the area and saw the faint trail of broken
grass that headed toward the bigger stream.
He followed this trail and saw where the
tracks vanished into the water. But had the
tracks necessarily been made by the horses

of Hovey and Silence? Any transient cow-puncher with a pack horse could have made the same tracks.

Nathan retraced his steps to the grazed area and began another circle, walking slowly under the sober gazes of the Boomers. There had to be some message here from Silence, intentional or unintentional. Reconstructing what probably happened, Nathan was reasonably sure that Hovey began to travel immediately after he reached the horses, so as to put distance between himself and the Boomer camp. If he saddled in darkness, he would have first bound Silence with his lariat. Surely she would have had the opportunity to leave a mark or a sign indicating she had been here.

But what could she leave? Nathan wondered, as he slowly tramped the area in ever-smaller circles. As his glance swept back and forth, he caught out of the corner of his eye an unfamiliar color in the trampled grass. Moving over to it, he bent down and picked up a bar of tan soap and when he had it in his hands, his heart leaped in excitement. He was certain that this was the bar of soap she had used in washing up last night.

Then he turned it over and smiled. There, scratched on the soap by a fingernail was the crude letter "S."

142

Nathan moved over to the two Boomers and showed them what he had found, and asked them to report his finding to Cap. As for himself, he was going to try to pick up the tracks while he still had some daylight.

Alone now Nathan put his horse into the stream and headed north up it, watching both sides of the bank for any sign of Hovey's horses leaving the stream. He passed occasional bunches of cattle that spooked away from him, then halted and regarded him curiously.

As Nathan moved up the stream, he began to comprehend the hopelessness of picking up the tracks. Cattle had watered here all day, crumbling down the banks and leaving deep water-filled hoofprints. Putting himself in Hovey's place, he knew what he would have done; he would have kept to the stream until he spotted a sizable bunch of cattle, then he would have circled them and driven them back over his tracks, obliterating them. After that he was free to move anywhere on the prairie. Just before dark, Nathan gave up. Ahead of him to the north he could see the flicker of lightning which presaged a storm. He turned now and headed back for camp.

Cap had finished his lonely supper when Nathan turned his horse into the corral and tramped up to the wagon. Cap looked at Nathan, saw no news in his sober face and then moved over to the stove and lifted Nathan's graniteware plate of food to the table.

After eating, Nathan rose, washed his plate and fork and then came back to the table where Cap was seated. The bar of soap which had been delivered to Cap and which he had carried in his pocket now rested in the middle of the table.

"Do you think she's all right, Nathan?"

"I've been thinking. If he wanted to harm her, he would have done it and left her. But it looks like he wants to keep her."

"Why, he can't! When word gets out what's happened, he'll be found and arrested! You don't steal a girl and travel with her without being seen, especially if everybody's searching for you."

Nathan was bone-weary and the emotions he had experienced this day had mauled him more than any physical hardship. Overwhelming drowsiness came to him then and he pushed himself to his feet, hearing the distant drum of thunder.

"I don't know where he's taken her, Cap, but I'll find her and bring her back. I don't know how, but I'll find her."

☆5☆

It began to rain sometime in the night and by morning the Boomer camp was a mire. Only the men building fence continued to string their wire and the sound of hammering came from those buildings that were roofed. Otherwise, the camp lay idle and in confusion. Singly and in pairs the nonworking men came to Cap's wagon and conferred with him under the fly. They wanted to know what they could do to help find Silence and Cap could not tell them. The rain, he pointed out, would destroy any chance of tracking Hovey and Silence, and Nathan had discovered that even before the rain, it had been a near hopeless chance. That left the whole West to search.

Early this morning, Cap told them, Nathan had set out for Fort Reno to enlist the help of the Army and to spread the word of Hovey's cruel act. He had no idea if the Army, which certainly did not love them, would help, and even if they offered to aid, how would they go about it?

The Boomer men Cap talked to listened in silence and in sympathy. The enormity of the crime was close to incomprehensible to these simple folk. They had all heard that in faraway cities women were stolen and forced into brothels. Most of them had heard frontier stories of white women captured by Indians disappearing for years on end. But to have a girl snatched from their midst, under their very eyes, was almost beyond belief. Cap's dogged optimism had vanished and he could offer them no encouragement on this cheerless rainswept morning.

Down the way Will Racklin had closed his umbrella and pulled his chair into the tent. So far this morning, he had sold precisely two plugs of tobacco.

He was surprised then when Catherine Henry halted in the rain at his plank bar. She had a shawl over her head and a man's coat thrown around her shoulders. The sight of her brought a wariness to Racklin's face. He called out, "Come around the bar and get out of the rain, Miss Henry."

Catherine skirted the bar and in seconds stepped into the tent. Racklin bowed briefly and said, "What can I sell you this morning?"

"A little bit of conspiracy, if you have it," Catherine said drily. Without being invited, she sat down on the chair Racklin had just vacated, and regarded him with her usual boldness. Racklin slacked onto the cot, put

146

elbows on knees and said, "I wondered when you'd be around."

"I've been wondering the same about you."

"I can't leave the store. Besides, I can't talk around your brother and his wife."

Catherine smiled faintly. "If you had come, what would you have talked about?"

"Carter was Hovey, wasn't he?"

Catherine frowned. "Carter? Was that the name of the man you hid?"

Racklin nodded. "But his real name was Hovey, wasn't it."

"Describe him."

"Tall, thin, half bald, mean blue eyes."

"So he came himself," Catherine said. Suddenly she began to laugh uncontrollably and Racklin waited it out, staring at her as if she had gone mad.

"I don't find the humor in this that you do, Miss Henry."

"Call me Catherine, Will, because we're in something together and will be for a long time."

Ranklin scowled. "I don't understand."

"You damned well do," Catherine said. "You hid Hovey for money and put him in a position to kidnap the Frane girl. I approached you with money to hide him, although I didn't know it would be Hovey." She paused. "I've got a secret, you've got a

147

secret. If it gets out, you'll be kicked out of camp and my teaching job will be gone."

"I didn't know I was hiding Hovey!" Racklin said heatedly.

"But you hid him."

Racklin rose. "Why did you come here?"

Catherine surveyed him with quiet contempt. "For three spools of cotton thread — black, white, green."

Racklin said nothing, but moved back to his trade goods. Presently he appeared with the three spools of thread. Catherine rose and Racklin handed her the thread.

"That'll be seventy-five cents."

"Not to me, it won't," Catherine said. "I just opened a charge account."

Racklin understood her immediately and smiled, lifting a corner of his slack mouth. "A little blackmail, eh?"

"That's a crude way of putting it," Catherine Henry said.

Then without warning, Racklin threw his arms around her and he kissed her savagely and long. She fought to free her arms, but Racklin was too strong for her. When he was through mauling her lips with his, he freed her and stepped back. The slap she directed at his face was effortlessly brushed aside by him. Then Catherine scrubbed her lips with the sleeve of her dress, as if trying to clean herself.

"Not a word," Racklin said. "You're being blackmailed." He gave a mock bow. "Come often. I enjoyed that."

Catherine stalked out of the tent, offended, angry, but somehow excited. At least here was a man, even if he was a saloon-keeper. A few Boomer young men who had walked her out were shy, inarticulate and their tentative attempts at love-making were so ridiculous that they evoked laughter instead of tenderness. It had been a long time since she had been kissed, and if it hadn't been done so vengefully, she might have enjoyed it, she thought.

Back at the Henry wagon, Catherine deposited her purchase beside Mary, who was sleeping through the rainy morning, then moved over to the fire where the rain fell sputtering into the big heap of coals. With a stick she scraped away the coals, revealing a Dutch oven. With the same stick she lifted the lid and saw that the apple dumplings were done. Using her dress skirt as a pot holder, she lifted the oven, moved over to the big grub box and put the oven down. From the grub box she took a plate and with a spoon deftly transferred the dumplings to the plate and covered them with a clean towel. Afterward she set out down the muddy street with the dumplings, endeavoring to put the incident with

Racklin from her mind. Her scheme had back-fired, but only temporarily. Besides, it wasn't important in the light of her bigger project.

As she approached Cap's wagon, she saw that Cap was alone, seated at the table under the fly, jotting down something in a notebook. When she stepped under the fly, Cap rose courteously, and said, "Good morning, my dear."

Catherine wasn't misled by his affectionate greeting since he greeted any female from one to ninety in the same manner. It flattered them and indirectly made their husbands proud that he considered their womenfolk such close friends.

Catherine put the plate of dumplings on the table before she said, "Good morning, Cap. I brought you a little something."

Cap lifted the towel, regarded the dumplings and said, "You shouldn't have done that, Catherine. I'll make out all right, but I do thank you."

Only then did Catherine realize that her gift must have seemed to Cap like the gifts of food which were tendered to a family after the death of a member. Still, she didn't care how it looked since it would make her seem generous and deeply sympathetic.

"Have you eaten anything this morning?"

"I — I wasn't very hungry," Cap said dully.

"We'll fix that," Catherine said in a businesslike voice. She moved over to the still warm stove on the back of which rested a granite coffee pot. Flipping the lid, she saw it was two-thirds full of grounds. After putting wood in the stove, she moved over to the water barrel with the coffee pot and filled it with water, then returned to the stove with it. All the while Cap was watching her with silent protest in his eyes.

Now Catherine returned to the table. "You'll have dumplings and coffee for dinner, Cap, and now let's talk about supper."

"Please don't bother," Cap said quickly. "I can rustle up something."

"Something like bread, if you've got it." Catherine's tone was gently reproving. She looked about and saw a chest at the end of the bench. "Isn't that your grub box?" she asked, and without waiting for Cap's answer, she went over to it and opened it. As she was surveying its contents, Cap said, "Please don't bother, Catherine."

Catherine acted as if she hadn't heard him and then she said, "How does Indian pudding for supper sound to you?" She looked over at him with the expression of a wife trying to please a husband.

"Why, all right, but I wish you wouldn't bother." There was an earnestness in Cap's voice that told Catherine she might be pushing this too far, but it only made her more determined. She closed the lid of the grub box, came over to Cap and halted before him, hands on hips. "Now see here, Cap," she said in a kindly scolding voice. "You can't live hand to mouth day after day. Of course, your neighbors will feed you, but pretty soon you'd think it wasn't fair to them, wouldn't you?"

"Why, I hadn't thought of it. Yes, I would think it was unfair."

"All right, let me cook for you," Catherine said bluntly. "I'm not needed at our wagon and you haven't a woman to feed you. You can't live like some old miner out in the hills on pork and beans. You'd be sick in a week."

From the look of thoughtfulness that came into Cap's face, Catherine knew that Cap had given no thought to the future. She said hastily, "Just until Silence gets back to take care of you, Cap."

"Yes," Cap said, "she'll be back." He scowled and looked out at the drizzle which was making a soft murmur on the canvas fly. "Well, it would solve a nuisance, Catherine, but I want to pay you."

"We could talk about that later, but I hope we won't," Catherine said. "It's settled then, Cap." Then, before he could change his mind,

Catherine said, "I'll be over this evening and cook supper. Then we can go through your supplies so I can see what you have." She pulled the shawl up over her head and Cap rose.

"You're too kind to me, Catherine. I don't know how to thank you."

"Please don't try," Catherine said. "Goodby for now."

As Catherine stepped out into the rain and headed toward the dreariness of the Henry wagon, she felt a quiet elation. While she felt sorry for Silence and for whatever had happened to her, the fact remained that she was gone. In a few days, Catherine knew, Cap would come to depend on her. In a week, she would fit so snugly into Cap's life that he could not do without her. Then it would be up to her to show him that he could never do without her in his future and she was no kind of a woman if she couldn't prove it to him.

Lieutenant Milham had finished inspection of the stables and paid his usual compliments to Sergeant Macy, who saluted and excused himself for the afternoon guard mount. When he heard, "Sir," from behind him, he turned and regarded Corporal Harney.

"The major's compliments, Sir, and he

wishes to see you in his office."

"Right. Thanks, Harney."

Headquarters was a frame building and just beyond its entrance was a large anteroom with doors opening off it. Two desks were backed up against the rear wall, the smaller being Corporal Harney's and the other belonging to the officer of the day who was not in at the moment. The rear door on the left opened into Major Kelso's office. As he crossed the anteroom, Milham heard the rumble of Major Kelso's voice in conversation. Tucking his hat under his arm, Lieutenant Milham knocked on the door frame and was bid enter.

Major Kelso sat at the desk behind which was the flag and A Troop's guidon and standards. In spite of the many open windows, the room was wretchedly hot. Seated in the chair facing Kelso's desk was Cap Frane's Indian foster son, to whom Milham nodded pleasantly.

"Scott, pull up that other chair and sit down," the major said brusquely.

When Scott was seated alongside Nathan, Kelso continued. "We've just had a kidnapping dumped in our lap."

Scott frowned. "Who, Sir?"

"Cap Frane's girl."

That would be little Silence, Scott thought, and he felt an almost sickening wrench of emo-

154

tion. It simply couldn't be true that anyone would want to harm this pretty and mischievous girl. "What happened, Sir?"

"It seems Mr. Frane here set fire to our friend Hovey's shack. That was in payment for Hovey's stampede. To get even with the Boomers for firing his shack, Hovey waited at the wash house — bath house? — and kidnapped her. Their tracks indicated before the last rain that they were headed north. Is that right, Mr. Frane?"

"Yes, Sir. In our search for Silence we found where Hovey's horses had been staked out. They had a head start of the night and most of the day."

Milham looked puzzled. "But what's he going to do with her?"

Nathan shrugged eloquently. Milham continued, "Was there a ransom demand involved?"

"No, Sir. He took her at night and we didn't discover until next morning she was missing. There was no note left behind."

"And you're sure it's Hovey?"

"Not dead sure, Sir, but who else would want to strike at Cap through his daughter?"

Major Kelso said, "Whoever took her wore cowman's boots, Scott. That much they're sure of." Now Major Kelso picked up a pencil, examined it and threw it on the desk in dis-

155

gust. "Mr. Frane, we'll excuse you. If you would like, go over to Edmond's and drink some beer while we knock this around."

Nathan rose. "Thank you, Major." He nodded to Milham and moved out into the anteroom and through it.

"Why in the blasted hell did he come to me?" Major Kelso said explosively. "It seems we're nothing but a bunch of wet nurses for that Boomer outfit."

"Isn't this a job for civilians, Sir?"

"Of course, it is, but will civilians do it? No, Sir. Half the whites on this reservation are wanted outlaws, but are they ever picked up?"

Milham knew that the major didn't want an answer to his question; he was simply protesting at the Army's lot.

"Just how do I go about finding this girl?" Kelso said grimly. "Am I supposed to march my troops through the whole damn West, asking if anybody has seen the Frane girl?"

Major Kelso rose now, circled his desk and began to pace the floor, arms folded across his chest. "This is not our job," he said flatly and then looked at Milham. "But if we don't do it, who will?"

"I don't think it's possible to steal a woman and hide her, Sir."

"If it isn't possible, then how do you go

about finding her? Deploy troops? Where do you send them? By now Hovey could be half way to California with her, if he went that way." He asked irrelevantly, "Is the girl pretty?"

"Very."

"Do you think Hovey would harm her? Young Frane thinks he hit her when he took her from camp. If he hadn't, she would've screamed." Major Kelso stood lost in thought for a moment, then added, "It seems to me, if he'd do that, he'll do worse."

It seems so to me, too, Milham thought. He knew he should accept this possibility, but his mind refused it. He remembered her vividly, especially the impudent gray eyes. Again, it came to him, perhaps for the hundredth time that if he had met her in other circumstances and without a uniform they would have become fast friends. The thought that she or any other girl would have to submit to Hovey's force sickened him. But in the case of Silence, it was unthinkable. As toward himself, she had not only teased and humiliated and angered him, but in doing so, she had contrived in some strange way to endear herself to him. When he was older and a married man with a family, he hoped he would have a daughter like Silence — maddening, temperish, pretty, bright.

Milham said slowly, "Sir, there's an odd tie between me and that girl. You'll remember two years ago — or rather you won't, because you weren't stationed here. Then she was a stick of a girl who incited the Boomers against us. The rest of it you know from my reports."

Kelso said nothing, waiting, as Milham, staring out the window, nervously thumbed his mustache. Milham's glance returned to Kelso.

"She doesn't think I'm much of a man or we're much of an Army. I'd like to prove her wrong on both counts. Call it pride, if you want."

Major Kelso, his puzzled glance on his junior lieutenant, rounded the corner of his desk and sat down. "What are you getting at, Scott?"

"This, Sir." He leaned forward, elbows on knees. "A minute ago you said it wouldn't make sense to deploy troops to search for her."

"It doesn't."

Milham straightened up and said, "Then let me look for her alone."

Kelso opened his mouth to speak and then seemed to think better of it. He was silent in thought for a moment before he said, "Where will you look?"

"It's too early for me to tell, Sir. I'd like

158

to talk with young Frane, maybe persuade him to go with me. There's nothing to arouse curiosity in a single white man traveling with an Indian. On the other hand, let the smallest detail of troops in uniform move through the post gates and the word's out that the Army's coming. God knows how the word's passed on, but I can count on the fingers of one hand the number of times we've surprised the enemy in our campaigns in the West."

Major Kelso only grunted acknowledgment of the truth Scott spoke. He was fiddling with his pencil again, not looking at Scott. "You're suggesting detached service, are you, Scott?"

"Either that, or I've got some leave coming up."

Now Kelso did look at him. "You would spend your leave on this impossible search?"

"Every hour of it," Milham said promptly.

Now Major Kelso put down his pencil with such delicacy that it might have been some unimaginably fragile object, and Scott found himself holding his breath.

"It will be detached service, not leave, and God knows what reprimand I'll get if you don't turn up that Frane girl." He rose now. "You talk with young Frane and report your plans back to me." He smiled wryly. "If they can be called plans, that is."

★ ★ ★

Silence was never to remember exactly how she got through the first night after Hovey had taken her from camp. She regained consciousness with a blinding headache that made her certain her skull was broken and that this was the beginning process of a slow death. She remembered scratching her initial in the bar of soap that was in her pocket and tossing it out into the night as Hovey saddled the horses. She also remembered Hovey hoisting her astraddle a horse and tying her feet together with a rope drawn under the horse's belly. Later she was grateful for the rope even if it had chafed her ankles raw, for it had allowed her to doze off and on through that dismally painful night.

Sometime after sunup Hovey, who was riding ahead of her and leading her bridleless horse with a rope, reined in a little, coiling the rope as Silence's horse pulled even. From his saddlebag Hovey took out a piece of stale panbread and extended it to Silence who only shook her head. The offer of his canteen she accepted, for she was wildly thirsty. She caught Hovey regarding her head but she did not have to feel it to know what he was looking at. The blow had broken the skin, and the hair on the left side of her head was matted with dried blood. As she handed back the canteen Silence spoke for the first time since she had been abducted. "Where are you taking me?"

"Don't know yet," was Hovey's laconic reply.

"But *why* are you taking me?"

Hovey was drinking now and when he had drunk his fill he wiped his mouth with his sleeve end, capped the canteen, and said without looking at her, "Figure it out. It'll give you something to do." Then he moved his horse on ahead.

The water for some strange reason had seemed to ease her headache, at least enough so that she became aware of the prairie around her. It was broken by occasional clusters of trees and plum thickets, and she saw occasional bunches of cattle in the distance. She had no notion of where they were but she did know they were heading north under a broiling sun that forced her to tear a strip from her petticoat to tie around her head for protection. A little past midday Silence regretted that she had not accepted Hovey's earlier offer of bread, for she was very hungry, and too proud to admit it. Would her father follow her or could he? she wondered. Turning in the saddle she looked back at the tracks their horses left. The tall grass seemed to spring back in place even as she watched. Time and again Hovey veered to the left or right to ride close to grazing steers so as to mingle their tracks with those of the cattle. The land seemed to be tilting up to the north and presently they achieved a rocky ridge. Here Hovey turned east, following the course of the ridge until the rock bars petered out.

In midafternoon Silence saw a row of trees to the east which indicated a stream. Twenty minutes later they approached the trees and Silence saw several horses staked out in the shade of them. As they came closer, she saw two men rise from where they had been sitting against the trunk of a tree, put hands on hips and watch them.

Reining in, Hovey nodded to the two punchers, who were regarding Silence curiously. They were both around thirty, dirty and unshaven, and wearing what was almost the range uniform — cowman's boots, denim pants, cotton shirt, buttonless vest and faded Stetsons.

Hovey stepped out of the saddle and said, "Better saddle up, Bert. Curly, untie her and change horses." To Silence he said, "Take a walk. If you aren't back in five minutes, I'll come after you."

While Curly freed Silence and helped her to the ground, Hovey unsaddled. While Silence walked off Hovey reached in his bulging saddlebag. From it he drew out a cheap tablet and some envelopes which he had bought at

Edmond's in Reno. He also extracted a new pencil which he sharpened with his pocket knife. Afterwards, he sat cross-legged on the ground, tablet on knee, and began laboriously to write.

He was still at it when Curly returned with Silence's fresh horse and a new mount for Hovey. As Curly was saddling Hovey's mount, Silence returned and said to Curly, "I'm hungry."

Curly tilted his head toward the cold campfire. "There's beans in the skillet."

Silence went over to the fire and saw the beans were swimming in coagulated grease with a spoon sticking out of it. It was hardly an appetizing looking dish, but by now she was ravenous. As she crammed down the cold beans, Bert came up with a saddled horse and a loaded pack horse and halted beside Hovey. Presently Hovey rose, stuffed some paper in an envelope, sealed it and gave it to Bert. Silence heard him say, "Tell Pond to put that with the Boomer mail. Stay there and watch him do it."

A ransom letter, Silence thought immediately. What other communication would Hovey have with the Boomers? Did Hovey really think that there was money in the Boomer camp to ransom her? The little money that the Boomers arrived with had gone for fence wire and there wasn't a man in the camp, with the possible exception of Will Racklin, who wasn't deep in debt.

Bert accepted the letter, took off his hat, put the letter in it, put the hat back on, mounted and rode past Silence, heading east. He eyed her obliquely as he rode past as if he were grateful for the sight of a woman in this womanless land.

Curly now went back to one of the two remaining horses and began saddling it and Silence, finished with her meal, rose and went over to Hovey, who was putting a rope around the neck of her new mount.

Halting beside him, Silence said drily, "Was that a letter to my father?"

Hovey looked down at her with no surprise in his lean face. "Reckon so."

"You're not very bright," Silence said drily. "There isn't fifty dollars to ransom me in the whole camp."

For a moment Silence thought Hovey was going to smile, but he only said, "I'll wait and take it out in corn."

For the first time since Hovey had taken her, Silence felt anger instead of helplessness. He had not only kidnapped her but was now joking about the ransom. "When are you going to tell me where you're taking me?" she demanded.

Hovey was again laconic. "When we get there." Now he turned to her. "Don't get a notion you'll run away, Missy. At night you'll be staked out like a horse, with Curly and me taking turns watching you. If you try to break away, I'll get some rougher than I was with you last night. You can always ride with a broken arm."

"I believe you'd do it!" Silence said angrily.

"You better believe it."

Now Curly came up with his horse and Silence resignedly walked over to hers, mounted and let Curly rope her ankles again.

Again they headed north and Silence saw that while they had been eating, the thunderheads had been building up to the north. Even now faint flashes of lightning flickered on the horizon, and Silence, eyeing the clouds, felt a leaden hopelessness. All day she had entertained a faint but persistent belief that somehow, someone would be able to follow their tracks, but a storm would obliterate them. And with the storm would go all hope of rescue.

Even as she was thinking, she felt the first stirring of the chill ground breeze that traveled ahead of the storm.

It was late afternoon when Lieutenant Winfield Scott Milham, very much out of uniform, rode into the Boomer camp with Nathan. Milham looked like any cowman who had bought a new vest at Edmond's in Reno and, as custom dictated, had cut all the buttons off of it. The rest of his clothes, including the Stetson, were well-worn from a hundred weekend hunting trips away from the post with fellow officers. Even his lariat was soft and gray with use.

They turned their horses into the brush corral, fed them and then headed for the Frane wagon. Since his last visit, more buildings had gone up, Milham noticed, and Nathan pointed out the bath house which was the scene of Silence's kidnapping. On the ride from Reno Milham had grown to like this quiet young Indian with a wry sense of humor. Little by little Milham had learned Nathan Frane's story, and while Nathan never put it in words for him, he learned of Nathan's love for Silence Frane.

When they approached the Frane wagon, they saw Cap, who had got word of their arrival, standing under the fly waiting for them. Catherine Henry was busying herself over a pot on the stove and at sight of her Nathan swore under his breath. As they drew closer, Cap Frane regarded Milham with some puzzlement, and only belatedly recognized him.

"Well, Nathan, you travel in strange company. To what do we owe this honor, Lieutenant Milham?"

Nathan put in quickly, "He's going to help us find Silence, Cap."

Milham nodded both in greeting and in confirmation of Nathan's news, then took off his hat and wiped the sweat from his brow with his shirt sleeve, all the time watching for Cap's reaction.

"Then you're not here to move us?" Cap asked cautiously.

"Those weren't my orders, Sir. I believe you asked for help from Major Kelso in finding your daughter. That's why I'm here."

"And how do you propose to do it?"

Cap's tone of voice was irritable and, looking at him, Milham noticed the change in his appearance. The skin of his face was pale and slack and the circles under his red-rimmed eyes bespoke sleepless nights.

"I haven't the faintest notion, Sir."

Without speaking, Cap wheeled and climbed into the wagon. When Milham looked around him, he surprised Catherine Henry watching him. He nodded politely. Nathan was eyeing her with quiet hostility. That this woman would presume to replace Silence in the Frane household was obscurely offensive to him, although he supposed that Cap had to have someone to cook for him.

Cap climbed down out of the wagon, came over to Milham, and extended a worn and wrinkled envelope. From it Milham drew out a sheet of much handled tablet paper and unfolded it and read:

Cap, yore girl is safe. If you dont folow my orders she wont be. If you want to see her agin you pack up all yore Boomers and haul them back to the Kansas line. Leave everthin whair it is and get the hell out of thair. If you do ile bring yore girl to you after you cros the Kansas line. If you dont yule never see yore girl agin never. Dont try to look for her yule never find her. Now get off my gras pronto.

Yrs
J. Hovey

Yore bein wached.
Ile no.

Milham handed the note to Nathan and waited in silence while Nathan read it and then said quietly, "That son of a bitch."

Now Cap sat down on the bench before the table and gestured loosely to two chairs. Milham sat down, took off his hat and laid it on the table while Nathan remained standing, re-reading the letter.

"What do you propose to do, Captain Frane?" Milham asked.

"You mean, will I ask my people to move back to Kansas?" Cap asked slowly.

"Yes, I guess that's what I meant."

"You'd like it if I said yes, wouldn't you?"

"Yes. Since you're going to be moved in the end, why not move them now?"

Cap's elbows were on the table, his forearms flat on its top, and his hands were clasped together. Now Milham noted that Cap clasped and unclasped his hands almost with the rhythm of his heartbeat. "I have an answer to that, Lieutenant, that I searched deep into my soul for. First, we will not be moved. Second, I have no right to ask these good people to uproot their lives to help me in my misfortune."

Nathan said sharply, "Cap, Silence is your child!"

"I know, Nathan," Cap said gently, but already stubbornness was beginning to creep into his voice. "Silence is my only child and her loss is my sorrow. I must bear it alone."

"But you're not bearing it alone," Nathan said coldly. "What about Silence? Isn't she bearing sorrow?"

Milham felt a slow anger mingled with contempt for this man rising within him. He was appalled that any father, especially the father of a girl like Silence, would utter these words. He could not keep the grimness from his voice as he asked quietly, "Would they move if you asked them to?"

Cap didn't answer immediately, as if the question had never occurred to him. "Of course," he said with sublime arrogance, "but I cannot ask them."

"Maybe I could."

"You will not be allowed to — especially you. You're Army. You want us moved and you'll seize upon this sad occasion to move us. Sir, we're here to stay. Like Moses, I've led my people into this promised land. How can I betray them?"

Nathan said quickly, "So you're not betraying your own daughter? Are these people your blood? Silence is."

Cap flinched visibly and said almost in a whisper, "Ah, Nathan, you're cruel."

"Not a tenth as cruel as you are," Nathan retorted. He took a step toward Cap. "Why is it you don't want Silence back?" He inclined his head toward Catherine Henry whose back was to them but who was listening. "Is it that?"

Cap glanced at Catherine Henry and a flush mounted into his pale face. "Nathan, that's unworthy of you."

"But you don't want her back," Nathan insisted. "If you did, you could have her."

Cap sighed. "I wish I could make both of you understand. I have taken money from these people and from people in other states that I never saw. I promised them all land and I kept my promise." He made a sweeping inclusive gesture with his arm. "A town is building here, and it is surrounded by rich fields. My conscience will not allow me to go against my word and destroy it. It would be dishonorable, Nathan. Can't you understand that?"

"No, I can't."

"Then can you understand this? For going on ten years I've tried to get into these lands. Each time I was turned back. Now we can't be turned back. We're here to stay. You are asking me to submit to defeat again when I am victorious. I cannot and will not ask these good people to leave. As I said, my conscience will not allow it."

"You mean your goddamn vanity won't allow it. What does your precious conscience say about your daughter?" Nathan asked angrily.

"We won't quarrel about this any more," Cap said flatly. "What we should be talking about is how to find Silence."

"Why talk? You already know how," Nathan said bitterly. He turned, walked out from

under the fly and headed down the street between the wagons, a murdering rage within
him. The tolerant and deep affection in which
he had held Cap for these many years had
vanished in the last five minutes. The man
was inhuman. What it came down to was that
Cap was placing his own vanity above the life
of his daughter. In his school books he had
read of the Incas sacrificing their daughters
to appease the gods. Cap was doing the same
damned thing, with the dollar as his god,
Nathan thought.

Suddenly he halted. There was a question
he had forgotten to ask Cap. Had he called
a council meeting to tell the Boomers about
Hovey's proposition? He looked about him
and saw he was close to the Henrys' wagon.
Ed Henry, back from the fields, was just finishing washing up at the basin atop the grub
box.

Nathan turned to him as he straightened
up and began toweling his face. At sight of
Nathan, he gave a surly nod. Nathan was used
to the suspicion with which many of these settlers regarded him. He was, after all, a member of a race they would like to see wiped
from the face of the earth.

"Hello, Ed," Nathan said easily. "I just got
in from Reno. Is your sister working for us?"

"Just till Silence gets back."

"I just read Hovey's letter. Did Cap call a council meeting and read it?"

Ed shook his head in negation. "He didn't call a meeting, but a lot of us read it. Reckon they all know what it says."

"If we pull up and move back to Kansas, he'll give us Silence," Nathan said slowly. Then he asked bluntly, "Would you give up your homestead to save her life, Ed?"

Suddenly Ed Henry seemed unable to look at him and he did not answer.

Nathan said quietly, "Is a hundred and sixty acres of land worth more than a girl's life?"

Still Ed did not look at him. "You keep saying, her life. Hovey's not going to kill her."

"You guarantee that?"

"Well, is he?"

"I don't know, and you don't either, Ed. Are you willing to give up a couple of months' work to make sure he won't?"

Now Ed did look at him and there was anger in his eyes. "A couple of months' work ain't what I'd give up! I'd throw away a hundred and sixty acres of the finest land a man ever saw!"

"All right, would you throw it away?"

"I'm not crazy," Ed said scornfully. "I paid my money to Cap Frane and I got land for the first time in my life. I got a wife and a

173

baby coming. Give it up? No, Sir."

"Not even to get the girl back?"

Ed shook his head like a bull about to charge. "Look here, now. I'm sorry for Cap Frane and for his girl, but I made a business proposition with Cap. There was nothing in the papers that said I had to protect his family, but there is something in the Bible that says I have to protect my wife and kid. That's what I'm doing."

"Do the others feel the way you do?"

"Ask them," he said shortly, and he turned around to hang the towel on its nail on the wagon side.

Nathan went on down the rough street and within an hour he had talked to a dozen Boomers, men and women both. All of them felt sorry for Cap and sorrier for Silence. And all of them said in effect that it was cruelly unreasonable to expect them to give up their precious land to get Silence back. When Nathan pointed out that the Army would move them eventually, they all said they would fight the Army before giving up their land. Cap had done his work well, Nathan thought bitterly. Cap had insisted that his land sales be conducted in a businesslike manner and it had been accepted by these people as a business contract. They had land they had bought. They were not going to move for anybody.

As Nathan walked back dejectedly to the wagon, he knew the bitter taste of failure. He could understand the reasoning of these people. They wanted to protect the ones they loved. Trouble was, he wanted to protect the one he loved.

When he arrived at the wagon, Catherine Henry was dishing up supper and Nathan sat down in silence. Apparently Lieutenant Milham had satisfied Cap that the Army out in force could not find Silence, for Cap was through with his questioning about Army help.

After the men had finished eating, Catherine Henry ate, cleaned up and went back to the Henry wagon. Cap, on the verge of exhaustion, retired to the wagon, leaving Milham and Nathan alone in the soft glow of the lantern.

Quietly then, Nathan told Milham of the poll he had taken. Even if Cap asked them to pull stakes, they would refuse.

Milham listened without comment, staring at the lantern as Nathan talked. When Nathan was finished, Milham grimaced in disgust. "What's so stupid about the whole damned thing," he said, "is that they'll be moving. In the end they'll lose this land."

"But when will they be moved, Scott?"

"That's what we don't know," Milham said. "We can't leave the post undermanned, but even if our troops were called back from the field, there's still Washington to consider. They're rowing about Indian lands again in Congressional committees. Our orders from Headquarters Department of the Missouri is not to move until we are ordered to. That was after I reported my failure to move the Boomers."

"So it may be months?"

"We'll have troops in a month, but it's anybody's guess when the orders will come through."

Nathan said quietly, "I'm not going to wait."

"Neither am I," Milham said, and regarded Nathan soberly. "Did Hovey's letter suggest anything to you?"

Nathan shook his head. "Should it?"

"If the Boomers pull stakes, he'll deliver Silence at the Kansas line. If he intends to keep his promise, wouldn't he hold her somewhere within a day's ride of the line?"

Nathan nodded. "So we head north."

"Let's do some pretending, Nathan. Suppose you were Hovey and had to hold Silence captive. How would you do it? How would you get your sleep? You couldn't watch her every minute."

"Tie her up?"

"And stay awake wondering if she was

working the knots loose?"

"I guess I would."

"Would you keep her in the country where you were well known?"

"You think she's in Kansas then?"

"They tell me Hovey was a trail driver for a long time. He'd stay out of the reservation and away from the trail towns, wouldn't he?"

Again Nathan nodded. "Seems likely. But he wouldn't dare take her into any town. Didn't you say Major Kelso asked headquarters to get in touch with the marshal's office? Wouldn't they spread the word by telegraph?"

Milham nodded. "Then he'd duck the railroad towns."

"Why wouldn't he duck all towns?"

"Maybe he would, but once he's out of Indian territory, he'll be in reasonably settled country. I think our best bet would be to search the country that's a day's ride above the line and away from the trails and the trail towns."

"And ask everybody we see if they've seen them camped or riding, is that it?"

Milham grimaced in disgust. "That'll have to be it." Milham rose and glanced over at Racklin's tent bar where the kerosene flare was burning. "Let's have a nightcap, Nathan. Come on."

"We'll have a nightcap. Just sit down."

Nathan moved over to the grub box, took out two tin cups and vanished across the road into the darkness. Moments later, he returned with both cups half full of whiskey and set them on the table.

Milham looked at the whiskey in astonishment. "You got a bottle out there in the night?"

Nathan said cryptically, "Not a bottle — a barrel." He lifted his cup and said, "To the search."

☆6☆

After breakfast on this chill, overcast, windy morning, Will Racklin set about his daily chore of bottling a half dozen pints of whiskey. Because he had emptied a keg last night, he hunted up a bung starter and went back to the storage area. After wrenching the spigot from the empty barrel, he shifted some trade goods from another barrel to the top of the empty one. Finding the bung on the new barrel, he placed both hands on the far side of the barrel with the intention of felling it on its side. Bracing himself, he gave a mighty heave. The whiskey barrel came so easily that Racklin fell down, the barrel atop him.

After a few seconds of surprise, it came to Racklin that the barrel was empty, and he scrambled to his feet, cursing. He gave the barrel a kick and it rolled easily. Then, still cursing, he found a match in his pocket and struck it alight on the barrel. Rolling it toward him, he soon found the separation in the staves. *What in hell?* he wondered. Could this barrel have been damaged in loading or unloading? And why hadn't he caught it? At any rate, he was out not only the fifty dollars it had cost him, but the hundred and fifty he would have sold the whiskey for, all because of some clumsy teamster.

In the blackest of moods, Racklin tapped another barrel, filled his pint bottles and corked them, and took them out to the box under the plank bar. Since the sun was not out, Racklin didn't bother to unfurl his umbrella, but slacked into the chair, lighted his first cigar of the day, and then regarded the Frane wagon just as he had regarded it in the past. This morning, as usual, Catherine Henry was there, serving breakfast to Cap Frane. Racklin's original mild curiosity was turning into a consuming one. Was this charity, or neighborliness, or a job? Along with the rest of the camp, Will Racklin had observed that Catherine Henry had more than an idle interest in Cap Frane. Whether she was attracted to him by his prestige or whether she thought that being seen talking with him added to hers, Racklin didn't know.

He watched Cap rise from the table, put on his hat, say something to Catherine Henry and then disappear toward the creek where he was finishing his soddy. The empty whiskey barrel had left Racklin feeling ornery and now this orneriness pushed him into action. He could think of no better way of working off his anger than by hazing Catherine Henry.

Moving around the plank bar, he tramped down the near grassless street to Catherine, who was cleaning up the breakfast dishes under the fly.

"Morning, sweetheart."

Catherine Henry looked up from the stove, then looked about her to see if Racklin had been overheard. Returning her glance to him, she said coldly, "You can cut that out, fatty."

I lose one hundred and fifty dollars and get called fatty, all in one morning, Racklin thought. Not a humorless man, Racklin considered his self-pity and then smiled, not at Catherine Henry but at his ridiculous self. "Your company gone?" he asked.

"Yes, he's gone, but he wasn't my company."

"Oh. I thought you were the lady of this here manor."

Catherine Henry's beautiful eyes narrowed. "That's not funny. I work here."

"So I notice. Why?"

"Well, somebody has to do for Cap."

Racklin smiled. "So it's Cap now. No longer Captain." Racklin couldn't be positive, but he thought that Catherine blushed.

"Well, we're friends," Catherine said resentfully.

"So are we. We're kissing friends, but you

don't call me Will."

"I call you Willie, Willie."

Racklin swore at her and Catherine said smilingly, "Tut, tut, Willie."

"Is Cap paying you for working?"

"Not yet, but he will."

Racklin moved under the fly now, pulled out a chair and sat down. "You wouldn't have a cup of coffee, would you?"

"Not for you."

Catherine returned to her dishwashing and Racklin watched her. She was a handsome woman, he thought, and besides that, she was tough in a ladylike way. Bluntly, he asked without hesitation or embarrassment, "How did you get this job?"

Catherine's tone was businesslike as she answered. "With Silence gone, Cap didn't have anyone to cook for him. I've got time on my hands, so I offered."

"I put the word out a month ago that I wanted a woman to cook for me. Why did you choose Cap over me?"

Catherine looked up. "Cap deserves help and you don't. You sit on that — that broad behind of yours, selling booze and gypping women. At least Cap does an honest day's work."

"I think you like the old fraud," Racklin said slowly.

"Doesn't everybody?"

"Not enough to cook for him for no pay."

Catherine asked angrily, "What business is it of yours?"

Now Racklin smiled. "Why are you mad? Am I coming close to something you don't want to talk about?"

"Yes," Catherine flared.

"Oho! Another one!"

"Another what?"

Racklin tilted back in his chair and said easily, "Another woman after the money of an old widower."

Catherine looked at him for a long moment, then said softly, "Well?"

"You admit it then."

"Only to you, Willie. We have no secrets from each other, do we? But we have secrets from other people, don't we?"

Racklin nodded in agreement, then said, "By God, you don't lack for gall, do you?"

"I never have."

"You would never get away with it if Silence was here, would you?"

Catherine smiled knowingly and said in a soft voice, "That poor child. I'm *so* sorry she's gone."

Now both she and Racklin laughed.

"How's it going with Cap?" Racklin asked.

"Well, he's beginning to depend on me."

"It will take more than that."

Catherine looked at him steadily. "I've got more than that."

Now Racklin rose. "Well, happy hunting, my dear. If you get him, he's good for a lot of laughs. I wish you'd rewrite his speeches, though."

"If you don't think those speeches work, just look around you. Look at yourself."

Racklin shrugged. "Oh, they work all right, but I can guess how his proposal to you will go. Something like this." Now Racklin raised his voice to the timbre of Cap's voice: " 'My dear, would you care to join me in wedlock and live in this Promised Land surrounded by God-fearing farmers whose love for the soil knows no bounds? Say yea, say yea.' "

Even Catherine had to laugh, and now with a friendly wave of his hand, Racklin headed back for his tent.

Catherine Henry, still chuckling, watched Racklin's bearlike walk. He was pure scoundrel, but a rather engaging one, she thought. He was so dishonest he could see only dishonesty in others, as he had seen it in her. Oddly enough, she thought that even if she had no blackmail hold on him, he would not repeat this conversation to a living soul. He watered his whiskey, lied and cheated at cards. An admitted predatory female was a cousin to him in immorality, she supposed. He respected her dishonorable intentions.

Silence and Jess Hovey sat in the shade of a tree in a country lane at the outskirts of a small Kansas town. Silence had lost count of the days they had been riding, but she thought it was a week. During that time they had met no one.

Two mornings ago when Silence had mounted her horse and waited to be tied in the saddle, Hovey had said to Curly, "No more ropes. Put the bridle on." To Silence he said, "We're getting into settled country now, so you can ride free. Have you noticed your horse ain't much good?"

"How could I help but notice it?"

"Then don't get a notion to run away on him. I can catch you in a quarter of a mile and I'll drag you another quarter at the end of a rope."

"Yes, *Sir*," Silence had said. During the past days Silence had responded to Hovey's orders thusly, putting into the two words both mockery and irony. It had begun to gravel Hovey until Silence thought he would hit her and she intended to keep on until he did.

She still had no notion of where they were headed. By the cultivated fields and sod huts they could see at a distance, she supposed they were now in Kansas. For the past week she had been wet, tired, sleepy, baked, hungry and lonesome. Hovey had spoken to her seldom and only then to threaten her in his level, toneless voice. The man called Curly had been oddly considerate of her in spite of Hovey's derisive stare every time Curly showed her a small courtesy.

There was a new life ahead of her, Silence knew, and she wondered what it would be. Her father and his friends could never raise the money to ransom her. Then what was Hovey going to do with her? When the money didn't show up, would he kill her, turn her loose, or keep her with him? By now Silence knew that Hovey was entirely capable of murdering her. Four days ago, when they wakened at dawn, they discovered that the pack horse had broken its hobbles and was gone. Hovey, white with rage, had saddled his horse and ridden off to search for him. Five minutes later Silence had heard a gun shot. Presently Hovey had ridden back to camp, seemingly satisfied. That he would inconvenience himself and Curly, that he would destroy a sound horse to satisfy his temper appalled Silence. He would destroy anything that crossed him or got in his way and that included her, Silence knew. She was afraid of him as she had never been afraid of anything in her life, but he would never know it if she could help it.

Now the figure of Curly approaching in the distance seemed to dance in the heat waves of this noontime. As he came closer, Silence noted with surprise that he was carrying nothing. She had supposed that Hovey had sent him to town for grub of which they were in very short supply, but this didn't appear to be the case. Curly rode into the shade, dismounted, reached in his pocket, took something from it which Silence couldn't identify and handed it to Hovey, who held it in his palm and looked at it. Then Hovey tramped over and halted before her.

"Get up."

Silence rose and Hovey held out his hand and unfisted it. In his horny palm lay a ring.

"Put it on your left hand — it's a wedding ring."

"You're going to pretend I'm married?"

Hovey nodded. "To me. Put it on."

"Oh, no," Silence said. "That ring means something."

"It means I want you to pretend to be Mrs. Hovey."

"No."

The word was scarcely out of her mouth before Hovey clouted her with a heavy backhand swipe.

"Put it on," he said tonelessly, and he still

held out his hand with the ring in his palm.

Silence felt the blood from her split lip trickle down onto her chin. "I'll put it on," she said, "but if you try to treat me as your real wife, I'll kill you. If you put a hand on me except to hit me, I'll kill you." She took the ring, slipped it on her finger and then said matter-of-factly, "I think I'll kill you anyway."

"I'm scared," Hovey said. "Now get on your horse." As Silence mounted, Hovey walked back to Curly and said something Silence couldn't hear. Curly nodded and moved over to his horse. He mounted, waved furtively to Silence, then rode off in the direction from which they had come.

Hovey and Silence rode through the hot afternoon, occasionally skirting fenced fields and distant soddies. Toward dusk they came in sight of a small crossroads hamlet snugged under tall cottonwoods. To Silence's surprise, Hovey headed directly for it and she glanced at him. An excitement came to Silence then. This town meant people and people meant help. Why had Hovey taken elaborate pains to avoid people only to take her into a town?

As they approached the town, Silence waited for Hovey's inevitable threats if she made any sound, but they never came. Looking about her, Silence saw several frame and log houses before they rode into the four corners which held the two biggest buildings in town — a combined hardware and grocery store, and catercorner from it the Plains Saloon. Hovey turned right and now Silence scanned the long boardwalk under the wooden awning of the hardware store. A couple of saddled horses and a team and wagon faced the tie rail and beyond them on the boardwalk a couple of overalled farmers were seated in the store chairs talking.

As Hovey and Silence drew abreast them, the two men looked at the travelers and Silence knew it was now or never.

"Help me! Help me!" she shouted. "I'm being kidnapped!" As Hovey reached over for her reins, Silence vaulted out of the saddle and ran toward the two men who by now were on their feet.

"You've got to help me!" Silence cried as she ran between the tie rails and achieved the boardwalk. Hauling up before the two men, both middle-aged, she saw them looking at her in open-mouthed wonder. Turning, she saw that Hovey had leisurely turned his horse toward the tie rail, leading her own.

Turning back to the two farmers, the words rushed out of her. "He stole me from my father! He's held me prisoner for a week! I've been tied in the saddle so I couldn't escape."

189

Lifting her dress skirt a few inches she said, "Look at my ankles. See the rope burns? Oh, you've *got* to believe me!"

Both men looked at her ankles and shifted their glances to Hovey. "What's going on here, Mister?" one of them asked.

In reply, Hovey slowly raised his hand, index finger extended, and tapped his temple. "My wife is sick," he said quietly.

"I'm not your wife!" Silence shrilled. "I'm not married to you or anybody else!"

The farmer who had been silent so far asked brusquely, "Why you got a weddin' ring?"

Silence turned to him and said angrily, "He bought it in that last town! He made me put it on! Oh, believe me! Please believe me!"

Now Hovey dismounted, swung under the tie rail and came up to them. When he spoke, his voice held no ire, only sympathy. "Come, dear. In a few minutes you can rest."

"I'm not going with you! I'm going home!" To the two men, she said, "Help me! Please help me! Don't let him take me!"

Hovey reached out and grasped her by the upper arm and when she tried to pull away, his grip tightened. To the two men he said, "We lost our baby two months ago. She ain't been right in the head since."

"That's a lie!" Silence shouted furiously. "I'm not married and I never had a baby."

"Come, dear," Hovey said. "It's just down the street."

Now Silence was crying in her despair and fury. "What he's saying is all lies! Everything is a lie!"

Hovey said now to the two farmers, "We're heading up to the railroad towns for a doctor. I don't reckon a doctor can do much for her, but I want to do everything I can."

The two farmers looked at each other and then back at Hovey, nodding in sympathetic understanding.

"You'd best go with your husband, Lady. He'll look out for you."

"But he's not my husband! My name is Silence Frane. His is Jess Hovey! I tell you he's kidnapped me!"

Hovey slowly shook his head. "We came through Fort Reno but the Army doctor couldn't help her. But I'll find some doctor if I have to sell our horses and go to Kansas City." He turned to Silence. "Come, dear. You've got to rest. We can't bother these men any more." His grip on Silence's arm tightened until she cried out.

"You're hurting me, you cruel bastard!"

Shock came into the faces of the two farmers. If they needed further proof of her insanity, they had it. No woman in her right mind except a fancy lady would use words

191

like that, their expressions seemed to say. Now Hovey slowly swung her around away from the farmers and as they moved toward their horses, Hovey said over his shoulder, "Excuse us, my friends. She was never like this before the baby died."

Both men nodded in mute understanding and watched Hovey gently but firmly propel her to her horse and help her mount. When Silence glanced at the two men, she saw that one of the stores' doorways held half a dozen people, both men and women whom she thought had overheard part of this exchange. She called out to them, "Help me! He's kidnapped me!"

The people in the doorway looked at the two farmers and Silence, in despair, saw the two men shake their heads.

Now Hovey took the reins of her horse, mounted his own and led her horse down the dusty street.

Looking back, Silence saw several people collected around the two farmers. She knew with the bitterness of despair that they were telling of their encounter with the girl who had been driven insane by the loss of her only child. Now too late she worked off her ring and threw it in the dust. Hovey only smiled. They passed the feed stable and blacksmith shop and then a small white box of a church before Hovey reined up in front of a paint-peeled, two-story frame house. Hovey dropped the reins of her horse and dismounted.

"Get down."

Silence looked at the house with distaste and then dismounted at the stone stepping block. "Is this where you're taking me?"

"Come along."

Hovey led the way up the boardwalk onto the porch where he knocked loudly on the door frame. Silence heard someone moving inside and then in the doorway appeared a woman. She was fortyish, a raddled blond in a sleazy, food-spotted blue dress.

She said in a cigarette-husky voice, "Well, you finally got here, Jess," but all the time she was looking at Silence in hard appraisal.

"This is the girl I said I'd bring, Beth," Hovey said. "She's got a funny name. It's Silence." To Silence he said, "This is Beth Majors."

Beth nodded curtly and Silence said nothing. Stepping back, Beth said, "Come in."

"No. Why are you taking me here?" To Beth, Silence said, "He's kidnapped me."

"I know, dearie," Beth said indifferently. "He wrote me he was going to, and he usually does what he says he'll do."

It took Milham and Nathan five days to dis-

193

cover the hopelessness of their search. Nobody they met, neither Indian, trail hand nor farmer, neither man, woman nor child, had seen a fifty-year-old, blue-eyed man in the company of an eighteen-year-old, dark-haired, pretty girl.

In the late afternoon they rode into the dusty trail town of Caldwell. They went immediately to the marshal's office, which was located in the front corner of the frame courthouse jammed in among other false-front buildings on Grant Street.

Marshal Tom Eldridge was laconic, taciturn and unhelpful. Yes, he knew Hovey, but he hadn't seen him. No, he wasn't making any special search. Where the hell would he start? He'd passed word to the stage drivers to be on the lookout, but they never saw anything except the rumps of their horses. Besides Hovey was unlikely to advertise his whereabouts by stopping at a stage station. Yes, the marshal supposed that all the railroad towns had got the same message he got, but what about the towns that weren't on the telegraph line? What if people *had* seen Hovey and the girl? the marshal continued in a discouraged voice. They wouldn't know Hovey was wanted. Probably never saw a lawman all year. Since Hovey was in the cattle business, he'd show up in one of the trail towns eventually and probably disclaim any knowledge of the girl. Forget the whole thing and let the law take its course. It would be slow, but they would get him eventually.

All the marshal said held words of wisdom, Milham supposed, as he and Nathan entered the barroom in the Caldwell House. It was too early in the summer for the rioting sprees of the trail hands so the saloon was nearly deserted. Milham and Nathan ordered beers, took them to a table and slacked into chairs. They both drank thirstily, then Nathan rose and got another pair of beers. When he was seated, Milham tilted back in his chair and gloomily regarded Nathan. "We could keep this up for a year, for five years, for ten."

Nathan nodded. "If we have to."

Now Milham settled his chair on all four legs and folded his arms on the table. "Do we have to, though?" he asked slowly. "I keep thinking of Hovey's letter. It said, 'Yore bein wached.' All right, who's watching?"

"Likely Hovey's riders."

"So if the Boomers move, they would get word to Hovey. In other words, they know where he is."

"I don't reckon you could beat it out of them. Is that what you were thinking?" Nathan asked.

"No. Here's what I was thinking."

★ ★ ★

Next morning Nathan and Lieutenant Milham headed back to the Strip. They camped off the trail that night and at midday reached the Pond Creek Stage Station which consisted of a frame house, log corrals and barns which sat just to the north of the tree-lined Pond Creek.

Because Milham knew Pond and didn't want to be recognized, he sent Nathan into the stage station while he circled the house and waited in the trees. Presently Nathan returned, dismounted, led his horse to the creek and then returned to where Milham was waiting.

Squatting down on his heels facing Milham, Nathan said, "Hovey's crew uses the station as a post office, just like we do. They haven't been around for a couple of weeks. Pond says he thinks that after the fire Hovey traded some beef to the Mineral Wells outfit for the use of a line shack that's west. About ten miles, he said."

"That's pretty vague."

"It's on the Salt Fork."

Milham rose and Nathan went back to the creek for his horse. Together they headed west under a blasting sun and presently picked up the Salt Fork of the Arkansas which they paralleled.

Conversation was a little shy on this ride, for both men were wondering if Milham's scheme would work. If it didn't, Milham thought wryly, he might just as well go home and put on his soldier suit again. Supposing it didn't work, what was going to happen to Silence? Since the Boomers wouldn't move of themselves and since the Army couldn't move them immediately, Hovey would have to keep Silence. But how would he keep her? And what would he do with her when he found that her kidnapping had resulted in nothing at all? Wouldn't he want revenge on Cap and wouldn't he have the instrument of revenge in Silence? It would be simple enough under the threat of violence to force her to marry him. It would be equally simple to sell her to a fancy house in any of the trail towns. To abandon her would be dangerous for, of course, she was the evidence of her kidnapping. Milham had heard and believed that many a girl answering advertisements in the eastern newspapers had come West under the impression that they would meet prospective husbands or find jobs as servants, waitresses, cooks or laundresses. And many of them wound up in cribs. The thought of that fate for Silence was unbearable.

In late afternoon they came on a shack among the cottonwoods on the river bottom that was as sorry as any Milham had ever seen. A huge cottonwood had been felled and out of this single tree a twelve-by-eight foot shack had been built, its trunk forming the five-foot walls, its branches sodded over to form the roof. A pasture was fenced with new wire and a log lean-to provided stock shelter. In the pasture were half a dozen horses and while Milham examined the interior of the shack, Nathan rode into the pasture to identify the brands on the horses. Upon his return he told Milham that the stock was branded Diamond H — Hovey's brand.

It was close to dusk when a rider appeared from the west. He reined up a good distance from the shack, observing the two horses and the two men who had risen at sight of him. Lifting his rifle from its saddle scabbard, he laid it across his lap and rode up to the shack where Milham and Nathan were waiting.

He was Bert, Hovey's hand who had delivered the ransom letter to the Pond Creek station. He was, Milham thought, unnecessarily dirty, even for a cowman; his hair was so long it hid the collar of his filthy shirt and almost covered his ears; his beard, whorled at the corners of his mouth, was shiny with grease. He surveyed them with eyes of the palest amber, which reminded Milham of a wary cat.

"We're looking for a Jess Hovey," Milham said.

"Look somewhere else."

"This is the Diamond H, isn't it?"

Bert thought about that a moment and decided he couldn't deny the brand on his horse and the other horses, so he nodded.

"Then Jess Hovey owns this outfit, doesn't he?"

Bert nodded. "He ain't here."

"Where do I find him?"

"I don't know."

Milham said patiently, "Look here. I know Hovey's in trouble and I don't give any part of a damn. I just want to do business with him."

Warily Bert dismounted, rifle still in hand. Now he squatted beside his horse, leaning on his rifle which was upright between his knees.

"Who might you be?"

"John Weaver, originally from Ithaca, New York." He nodded in Nathan's direction. "This is my guide that I picked up in Fort Reno."

"Guide," Bert echoed. "Can't you find your way around alone?" His tone was derisive, close to hostile.

"No, I can't," Milham said equably. "I'm new here, but I won't be long. I want to talk with Hovey."

"If he was here, what would you talk to him about?" Bert asked.

"Money."

"Money for what?"

"For his grass lease."

Bert reached out, plucked a stem of grass, raised it to his mouth and began nibbling on it, watching Milham with careful consideration. "He ain't here."

"Damn it, I know that! Where'll I find him?"

"He ain't here," Bert replied.

Milham regarded him coolly. "My good man, what's your name?"

"John Smith."

Milham shrugged and said, "It really doesn't matter. I think I can describe you to Hovey when I see him. I'll tell him you're the man who tried to lose him seventy-five thousand dollars."

Milham regarded him long enough to see his eyes widen, then he turned and started for his horse.

"Hold on," Bert said, but Milham didn't even pause in his stride. Now Bert rose, and in the same movement cocked his rifle. "I said, hold on."

Milham halted and turned to look at him.

"How do I know you're who you say you are?" Bert asked warily.

200

Milham regarded him for several moments and then he said contemptuously, "You don't. Still, my commission agent in Reno tells me Hovey paid seven hundred dollars to the Indians last year for a grass lease on roughly thirty thousand acres. His north boundary is Officer Creek; his west boundary is the Mineral Wells Cattle Company fence; his south boundary is the Cheyenne-Arapaho reservation; his east boundary is Little Piney Creek. He runs seven hundred head of double-wintered steers. I'm in a position to offer him or anybody else seventy-five thousand dollars for grass and cattle to set up a business." He paused. "That's all you need to know about me. My name could be John Smith, too, for all it matters to you."

Again he turned and started for his horse and this time Nathan started for his horse, too. He had tipped his hole card now, Milham thought, and if it didn't take the pot, nothing would. His information regarding the number of acres Hovey leased, the amount he paid the Indians, the number of cattle he owned, was accurate and had been assembled at Major Kelso's orders as a matter of information for the Army. Milham hoped it would lessen this trail hand's suspicion.

Reaching his horse, he stepped into the saddle and waited for Nathan to mount. Now

201

Bert walked slowly toward him, saying, "Where'd you find out all that about Hovey?"

Milham looked at him with contempt. "At Fort Reno. Where else? I'm not about to offer seventy-five thousand dollars for a pig in a poke. I also know who owns the Mineral Wells Cattle Company, how much graze they lease, and the number of cattle they run. I have the same information on the Cherokee Outlet Company."

Bert studied him in silence. "You mean you want to buy out Hovey?"

"I thought I made that clear. When I do, you'll be the first hand to be discharged."

"I wouldn't work for you."

"That's for damn sure. Once I get in touch with Hovey, I don't think you'll be working for him either."

"You ain't a law man?"

Milham sighed and said patiently, "Look. I'm from Ithaca, New York. How could I be a law man here?"

"Them ain't dude clothes."

"Bought in Wyoming, used there and in Montana. Am I supposed to wear tails and a top hat in your country?"

Bert looked down at the ground and began kicking the tufted grass and Milham knew the rider was considering his sorry dilemma. Hovey had undoubtedly sworn to kill him if he revealed the hideout. On the other hand, if Hovey learned that a prospective buyer had been turned away, his job was gone.

Now for the first time Nathan spoke. "They don't like money here, Mr. Weaver. Maybe somebody else likes it."

"Right you are," Milham said, and put his horse in motion.

"Hold on," Bert said quickly. When Milham reined up and regarded him, Bert came closer. "Send that Injun away," he said quietly.

Milham looked at Nathan and said soberly, "Running Bear, we want to talk privately."

Nathan had to turn his head to hide the smile. Dutifully he put spurs to his horse and rode off into the shade of the trees.

Now Bert said, "What's the talk in Reno? Is there a reward out for Hovey?"

"If so, I didn't hear it."

"If I tell you where he is, you going to tell that damn Injun?"

"You'd rather I didn't?"

Bert snorted. "Hell, if there's a reward out for Hovey, he could start bounty huntin'. 'S far's that goes, you could, too."

Milham said coldly, "Now consider this carefully. I'm trying to *spend* money, not *earn* it. All I want is Hovey's signature on a paper, not his head on a platter."

His irony was lost on Bert who asked now,

"Do you know why they're lookin' for Jess?"

"I know only what I heard. He ran away with a woman and her father's out to get him."

"Is that the talk in Reno?"

Milham nodded.

"Well, he's up in Kansas."

Milham said nothing. Bert said nothing. They simply looked at each other and presently Milham spoke. "So are a lot of other people."

"In Alma," Bert said reluctantly. "Look up Beth Majors."

Milham tried to hide the exultation he felt as he asked calmly, "Where would Alma be?"

"In Kansas, this side of the Arkansas, is what he said. Ask around."

"Thank you," Milham said civilly. "Now I can dismiss my Indian."

"Hell, shoot him. The only good —"

"I know, a dead one." Milham touched spurs to his horse, picked up Nathan and they headed east.

☆7☆

Beth Majors had a curious history, Silence was to learn in the time she spent at Beth's house. Silence's first look at Beth told her Beth was tough, but with a kind of toughness Silence had never come up against. The Boomer women Silence had grown up with were physically tough and some of them were successful enough nags to bully husbands, but Beth had a gutter toughness that appalled Silence.

Beth, it came out, had been born into a miserably poor Irish family in an eastern factory town, had quit school at a tender age to go on the streets, only to end up in a house of correction. By the time she got out, her mother was dead of drink and her father had deserted the six children who, with no central core of family, scattered to the four winds. Beth went back to the only trade she knew and presently was contacted in a brothel by a man who was rounding up girls for the railroad construction-gang tent cribs. As the railroads moved on, trail towns built up behind them to receive Texas cattle and Texas cowboys. Tired of being ever on the move and tired of the construction crews who mostly couldn't speak English, Beth found a house in one of the railroad towns that would take her.

This was where Hovey met her, along with his friends, on their annual spree after fall shipping.

At the time she was pretty enough, so that the other girls in the brothel envied and hated her. What fascinated Hovey about her was her unadorned greed. While the other girls spent their money on clothes, jewelry and booze, Beth learned the honest card games and dealers in town and slowly began to build her stake. When Hovey asked her why, she had said, "Look at the other girls. A few years, they won't be good for the only thing they're good for. Not me."

Beth was to leave her profession sooner than she expected. Tom Majors, an old trail friend of Hovey's who had been crippled in a trail accident, was escorted into the parlor by Hovey one night and introduced to Beth. Shortly, Tom Majors' whiskey had made her a little drunk. In his day Tom had been a talented hell raiser and that night, as Beth put it to Silence, "He raised hell and then tilted it." A few days later Beth was married to Tom Majors, among the celebrating girls who were glad to get rid of deadly competition.

With what Tom Majors had saved, they bought an option on a small stage line which ran south from the railroad and into Arkansas. Majors knew horses and Beth, in her drive for money, had learned from a succession of madams a rudimentary bookkeeping. They both decided to choose a town on the stage line where they were not known and which would be free of trail hand acquaintances.

They prospered until Tom was gunned down on one of his drinking sprees and Beth took over management of the line. In a few years she managed to sell it for a tidy profit and then placed the money in the care of Jess Hovey who detoured by their place each fall on his return from Texas.

So Beth had climbed from the squalor of the slum to this respectable, unassuming home in a small Kansas town. She was still greedy, still foul-mouthed, still tough, but she at last had freed herself of all male bondage.

The first days Silence had spent there, Beth had never let her out of her sight and at night she locked her into a sweltering room under the eaves whose single window was too small for even Silence to climb through.

Hovey came and went, on what business Silence didn't know. If it hadn't been for Beth, Silence would have wondered if she had become invisible, since Hovey neither looked at, nor spoke to her. She was something he stepped around on his way in and out. One thing she did learn; Hovey was afraid of pursuit. If trouble happened while he was away, Beth was to pull down her bedroom window shade as warning of danger. But who would pursue him, Silence wondered. Who knew he was here?

At first, Silence patiently began to consider the possibility of escape. Beth Majors' habits had a certain pattern. She rose late, let Silence out, and together they had breakfast. Beth's first drink of the day was at midmorning when she got out the cards and set up a complicated game of patience. When Silence, out of boredom, proposed that Beth teach her card games, Beth welcomed the chance. The midday meal was sketchy if Hovey wasn't there. Beth continued to drink during the day, but it was while she was getting supper that the really serious drinking started. Since there was nothing in the house to read, no sewing to do, no clothes to mend, Silence was at her wit's end to occupy herself. Cooking was the only woman's chore she could work at, so in the evenings while Beth drank and chatted, Silence made pies, rolls and cakes until there was scarcely shelf room for them.

As the evening progressed, Beth would get drunker, her red hair awry, her face even redder. But she never drank so much that she couldn't escort Silence up to her room and lock it. Silence knew if she could get out of her room during the night, Beth's senses would be too fogged by alcohol for her to even wake up.

One evening Silence thought to test Beth's alertness. She was cleaning up after a cooking session, washing pans and spoons, and the water in the dishpan was clotted with dough. Glancing over at Beth, Silence saw she was vacantly munching on a still warm roll whose butter was dripping down the corners of her mouth. Silence lifted the pan but instead of going to the sink, she went through the back door and onto the back porch where she was forbidden to be at night. Moving toward the back steps, she saw her shadow appear out of the black night ahead of her. She turned and saw Beth in the doorway, a pistol in her right hand, a lamp in her left.

"I brought my own light so I'd be sure to hit you," Beth said coldly. "Get back in here."

Silence returned to the kitchen and dumped the water in the sink, her heart pounding.

To her back Beth said in the same cold voice that was suddenly not drunk at all, "Dearie, you don't understand about me and money. You walk out of here and I've lost money.

I'll shoot you to keep from losing it. Don't ever forget."

And she would shoot, Silence thought.

Over the days Silence never ceased thinking of escape. Supposing she could miraculously break away from Beth. If she could make it down the street to the store or the saloon, she would only be gently captured and kindly returned as poor Hovey's lunatic wife. If she made the saloon, she would run into Hovey playing cards or if not Hovey himself, then men who had heard the story of her demented state. The whole town would be her captors. No, her escape could not involve people. It would have to be accomplished alone. Suppose she was lucky enough to break out, lucky enough to steal a horse, then where would she go? She didn't even know where she was.

She had, however, sorted out one persistent event that broke the series of dreary evenings. It was the passing in the street of the north-bound stage. It was the signal for Beth to drain her glass, rise and order Silence up to her cot under the eaves. As she reflected on every possible means of escape, it came to Silence with growing conviction that the stage was her answer. At the end of the stage line would be a town where she could learn where she was. Trouble was, the stage driver would know her story and turn her over again to

Hovey. Also, she would not have money for stage fare, even if she could break out. When she came up with no answer to this insoluble problem, she always thought back to her friends and family and despaired anew. She was certain that by now they had given up hunting her. If she was ever to see them again, then she must hunt them. But how?

This evening she was rolling out dough for cookies that she would bake tomorrow when the stage rolled down the street past the house, its harness jangling, the sound of its rumbling wheels muffled by the deep dust.

"Time for bed, dearie," Beth said.

A thought came to Silence then as she held the handles of the rolling pin in either hand. It was a thought that terrified her, and she put down the pin quickly.

"I know," Silence said. She slipped the cookie dough into a pan, and leaving it on the table, she slid the rolling pin in the drawer and turned docilely to go to bed. Beth, she saw, was standing and waiting.

Once in her hot, dust-smelling room, Silence lay down on the cot, her heart still racing. Would she have the courage to do it? It would take timing and luck, and failure would be disaster. *What's this if it isn't disaster?* she thought.

The next day Silence began a sly and roundabout questioning of Beth. Why had she and Tom Majors chosen this town to live in? Silence began. Obviously they had no friends because since she had been here nobody had come to the house. One question about the town led to another, and before the afternoon was over, Silence had a fair idea of the town's businesses and the men who ran them. But what was most important, she had a very certain knowledge of where and how the stage changed horses.

Hovey came in for his supper and Silence, closely observing him, thought he seemed preoccupied, even worried. His shortness with Beth at the table bore that out. He left without even his usual brusque good-by and Silence wondered if the protracted wait for the ransom money was beginning to get on his nerves. Didn't he know by now that Cap couldn't come up with any money? More important, what would Hovey do to her when this money didn't come?

It seemed to Silence this evening that what was slowly developing into a plan must become a perfected plan tonight. All the ingredients of her plan were here; all it needed was the courage she didn't think she had until now.

The after-supper routine was as usual. Luckily, Hovey had put a dent in the stock of baked goods today and Silence, under

Beth's usual surveillance, brought out mixing bowls and paraphernalia, flour and lard.

"I'm going to make something special tonight," Silence said.

From her chair Beth said boredly, "I wish to God you would ease up on that stuff. I'm getting a belly on me like a pregnant mule."

"It's something to do," Silence said meekly.

"Every night you get this kitchen hotter than the hubs of hell."

"Well, it's the coolest time of day," Silence countered. "Anyway, I won't be long."

She had to time this just right. Whatever she concocted had to be so unusual that it would be worth calling Beth over to examine. Quickly she whipped up a white cake and slipped it into the oven. While it was baking, she made a pan of caramel sauce. As time passed a feeling of both dread and excitement grew within her. She was a fool to try this, but she was also a hopeless coward if she didn't.

When the cake was finished, Silence took it to the table, turned it out, let it cool a few minutes and then, watching the clock, she went over to the stove and brought back the pan of cooling caramel sauce. Now with a spoon she dipped up caramel sauce and leaning over the cake, began to dribble a thin stream of the sauce onto the cake. Slowly she drew the outlines of a long angular head. She put in the eyes, a vertical line for the nose, a horizontal line for the mouth and another vertical line for the cleft in the chin. Atop the head she put a broad-brimmed Stetson that she colored solid with caramel.

Now glancing at the clock she thought it was about time. Stealthily then she opened the table drawer and took out the heavy wooden rolling pin which she held against her leg, partially hiding it in the folds of her dress skirt. With a final glance at the clock, she said in simulated enthusiasm, "Oh, look at what I've made, Beth. Come look."

"Bring it over," Beth ordered. Her speech, Silence noted, was as usual at this time of the evening, slurred with alcohol.

"I can't," Silence protested. "The cake's too hot and if I lift it, it'll crack and spoil this."

"Oh, for God's sake," Beth complained. She eased herself to her feet and crossed the kitchen in a dignified lurch. Pausing just short of the table, she glanced at the cake and then at Silence. "My God, you're like a kid painting Easter eggs."

"No," Silence protested. "You haven't looked at it. I mean, look closer. Don't you recognize what it is and who it is?" Now Beth came up to the table and leaned over to examine the drawing.

"Well, by God —" was all that she got out before Silence savagely swung the rolling pin across Beth's head. Beth's face smashed down into the cake and then she toppled sideways and fell on her back.

Silence did not even bother to look at her. She went out the back door into the cooling night and headed for the alley behind the chicken house and turned right. There she halted long enough to let her eyes accustom themselves to the darkness and then hurried down the alley toward the center of town. At the cross street she looked in both directions. The traffic of the town had slacked off for the day and as she walked across the street heading for the opposite alley, she saw that the only light visible was at the brightly lit Plains Saloon. Achieving the opposite alley, she hurried down it until she reached the rear of the livery stable. Across the alley from it horses that she could not see were snorting and moving inside the corral.

Slowly now, Silence stepped into the plank driveway of the stable and hugging the stalls tiptoed toward the street. Hanging to one side of the front archway entrance was a lantern whose light barely reached the first two stalls.

Quietly now, Silence moved forward. A stable cat sprawled out on the stable partition started to purr at her approach and the noise in this immense silence startled and alarmed her. Now Silence had reached the faint light thrown angling into the first stable. She moved into the shadow of the angle, then hugged the wall, her back to the street. Outside in the street she heard horses stomping and rattling their harness. A sudden voice startlingly close to her began to curse the restive horses without much enthusiasm. This, Silence knew, was the team change waiting for the arrival of the stage.

The minutes dragged on and Silence's wild impatience increased. What if Beth woke up and gave the alarm? What if the stage delayed long enough to give Hovey time to wander into Beth's and discover her? Then, as if in answer to her silent pleadings, she heard the familiar sound of the stage in the distance.

Silence had watched enough stage changes in her childhood to know the routine. Fresh teams already harnessed were waiting outside. Usually two hostlers made the change. One held the reins of the fresh teams while the other one unhooked the spent teams and drove them to the corral to unharness and turn them loose. The other hostler hooked up the fresh teams, handed the reins up to the driver and the stage was off. This town, Silence knew, was not an eating stop, so there would be little delay in the team change. It seemed, however, that there was only one hostler for this change since, if there had been two, there would have been idle talk during the wait. Somehow in the next few minutes, she had to get on the stage in the presence of two men, the driver and the hostler. She didn't know how to do it.

Now the stage was near and Silence could hear the rasp of the brake over the driver's shouted, "Whoa! damn you. Whoa!" Poking her head out into the centerway, Silence saw the sweating pair of teams pull into sight and then the stage appeared, stopping on the far side of the runway.

"Hi, Harv," the hostler called. The stage driver, a bearded man in a duster whose creases sifted dust at his every movement, had the disdain of his profession. He gave no greeting, only asked surlily, "Any passengers?"

Now the hostler drove his teams around the back of the stage as he called, "Nary a one." Then he added, "Hold the reins, Harv. They're a little salty tonight."

"Go between 'em and you'll likely get your head kicked off."

"I never have yet," the hostler replied.

Now was the time to act, Silence knew. Harv was holding two sets of reins and the hostler on the far side was unhooking the spent teams. The dust curtains of the stage were drawn and if it held passengers, they could not see her. Now she moved swiftly toward the canvas-covered rear boot and she felt naked in the glow from the lantern hanging beside the archway. Reaching the boot and in plain sight of anyone who chanced to be watching, she yanked the heavy harness strap loose from its buckle and lifted the canvas, praying that the boot would be empty. It was not empty, but neither was it full. Now Silence ducked into it, banging her knee on a sharp-cornered suitcase, afterwards letting the flap fall. There was no way she could buckle the flap from inside the boot, but she hoped this would go unnoticed. Inside the boot, Silence tried to arrange herself comfortably and failed. But it didn't bother her. She was almost free and she found herself holding her breath, waiting for the stage to start. Then she heard the driver's shout and the simultaneous crack of his whip and the stage shot forward with a lurch that almost threw Silence through the canvas.

I'm free, Silence exulted. I'll be miles away before they find Beth.

Now she settled back against the jolting luggage, the constant rumbling of the wheels music to her ears. At every turn they would put her far from Hovey and Beth.

It was useless to try and sleep, but she

wouldn't have wanted to even if she could have. Her thoughts were on what lay ahead of her and how she would meet the problems. The stage line, Beth had told her, terminated at a railroad town. Surely, if the town wasn't a county seat and didn't have a sheriff it would have a marshal to whom she could tell her story. In his ordinary line of duty the marshal would be required to get in touch with Cap, who would send someone up after her. The agony of these last weeks would then be over.

The stage had been rolling for perhaps half an hour when it slackened speed and finally came to an abrupt stop.

Another station stop? Silence wondered. She could hear voices, but could not make out what they were saying. Now she felt and heard the stage door slam. She supposed that the passengers were taking advantage of a stop-over to eat.

Then with the abruptness of a gun shot, the canvas flap of the boot was lifted. There to one side stood the driver holding up the canvas. Beside him, holding a lighted match, was Hovey.

"Well, by God," the driver said in wonder. "I swear I never knew she was in there."

Hovey nodded slightly and said, "Come, dear. We're going back home."

"So that's your crazy woman. She's right

purty," the driver said.

Something beyond despair engulfed Silence then. Hovey had already planted the story of his crazy woman with the driver, and to beg the man for help would be useless.

The match died and now Hovey took a step forward, grasped her wrist and said again, "Come, dear. We have a long ride ahead of us."

Silence climbed out and Hovey never released his grip on her wrist. In one last act of desperation, hoping that Hovey was as blinded as she was by the match light, she grabbed with her free hand at the gun in Hovey's holster. Instead of finding the gun butt, she found Hovey's fist covering it. Tightening his grip on her arm, Hovey swung her to the side away from the gun. "Thanks, driver. Sorry to hold you up. I'm lucky you didn't shoot at me."

"I'd a notion, all right, but I figured you'd shoot back," Harv said. Now he buckled down the boot canvas.

Swinging Silence in a half circle, Hovey led her firmly to his horse. After gathering the reins in his hand, he ordered her to mount. At the same time, Harv swung up on the stage, called, "Good luck with the lady, Mister," and shouted the team into motion. Now Hovey, still keeping the reins, swung up behind

Silence and he spurred his tired horse into a walk. The night was hot and moonless with a smell of growing crops that somehow deepened Silence's sadness.

"That was a pretty cute trick," Hovey said.

"What are you going to do with me?"

"Beat hell out of you and lock you in your room."

"Have you ever beat up anybody but a woman?" Silence asked bitterly.

For answer Hovey drove his fist into her lower back, bringing paralyzing pain.

"Just be quiet now."

As Will Racklin opened his tent flaps and stepped out to regard the bright sunny morning, he glanced down the street and saw that Catherine and Cap were breakfasting together under the fly. The sight of them irritated him as it had mornings past. In the last ten days, that hussy had progressed from being Cap's cook to his table companion. Shortly she would probably be his bed companion, too, and the thought of it rankled him.

She was a scheming, unprincipled woman, but he wondered if she knew what lay ahead of her if her plan succeeded. To be the second Mrs. Frane might in time make her a rich widow, for Cap, besides collecting the colonists' membership dues, had staked out several strategic lots in the townsite which was fast abuilding. But to earn her way to a rich widowhood, Catherine Henry must live with a teetotaling fool whose every word and action was either laughable or ridiculous. There was too much life and laughter in Catherine Henry to tolerate this dull fraud. To live with him she would have to become like him — windy, pompous, pious and mean in spirit.

While there was no guarantee that Cap Frane would wind up rich, the odds were that he might. Looking about him, Racklin saw that many of the future business buildings were close to completion. The McLaren brothers' huge covered warehouse, which was fed almost daily by freight wagons bringing in all manner of general goods and hardware, would be turned by the end of summer into a mercantile store that could service a much bigger town than this.

Racklin wondered if his hunch to go slowly and wait on events hadn't been a wrong one. If he had started along with the others to build a modest frame saloon which could be expanded, the building would be almost finished by now. It seemed to him that in the face of the construction that was turning this camp into a town the government might have to give in. He could still build, but what if one of these sly farmers with an almost finished building decided to turn it into a saloon instead of a home? Or what if he sold it to some outsider who would make a saloon out of it? The thought was depressing, and Racklin turned back to his after-breakfast chore of filling the bottles. The only thing that made his reveries tolerable was the fact that he was selling twice as much whiskey now as a month ago, thanks to the teamsters and freighters who could be relied upon to have a thirst.

After Racklin had filled his bottles and set them out and sold a couple of yards of lace edging to a sheepish farmer shopping for his wife, he slacked into his chair under the raised umbrella. Presently, Catherine Henry left the fly and headed his way. For the past week or so, she had taken to visiting him when her breakfast chores were done. They talked mostly of Cap and her progress toward matrimony. It was a little like those stories in the eastern magazines that Racklin had been told about. Each issue carried a short part of a longer story and they cut it off at the most exciting moment so the reader would buy the next issue, hating himself for being such a sucker. Racklin felt the same way about Catherine's romance, but he could not resist listening any more than she could resist telling him.

As Catherine approached, Racklin moved

into the tent and brought out another barrel chair and placed it beside his own.

"Good morning, Mrs. Frane," he called in a brassy voice.

"Be quiet, Will," Catherine hissed.

She came around the plank bar and took a chair.

"Well, has he got you scrubbing his back yet?"

"That's indecent," Catherine said in a proper tone of voice.

"So are you, come to that."

Catherine glanced at him in mild surprise. "My God, you sound as smug as he does. You must have been reading the Bible last night."

Racklin laughed without much enthusiasm and asked curiously, "Does he ever talk about Silence?"

"Only when he says he's going to pay me when she gets back."

"Does he really think she'll be back? Does he think she'll walk in here some fine day? If he doesn't hold out any hope of that siwash and Mr. Army finding her, how does he reckon she'll get here?"

Catherine only shrugged. The subject of Silence did not interest her.

"He's a fool," Racklin continued darkly.

Catherine looked at him appraisingly. "You sound angry."

Racklin shrugged. "Cradle-robbing men and grave-robbing women make me kind of sick."

"I thought you thought they were funny."

"I do. They're funny but they're sad, too. The cradle-robber is after something young. He wants to be young again and that's sad. But the young and pretty grave-robber is a vulture. That's sad, too."

"You pious bastard!" Catherine said angrily and looked away down the street. Then she straightened up in her chair and swiveled her head back to look at Racklin. "Do you see what I see?" she asked and tilted her head in the direction of the Frane wagon.

Racklin looked up and saw a cavalry officer, gauntlets tucked in his belt, standing under the fly looking about him. At that moment the triangle clanged out its harsh command to assemble. It went on interminably and when it ceased, Cap Frane stepped up beside the Army officer.

"Well, we have another go-around with the Army, it looks like," Racklin observed.

The camp was stirring with movement now as men and women left their work and children left their play to head toward the meeting grounds between the Frane wagon and the creek. Slowly the sound of builders' hammers died and now Racklin rose.

"This is a strange time to call a meeting, isn't it, Will?"

"Maybe Cap was told to call it," Racklin said dryly. "Come on, Mrs. Frane. Let's go see what your almost-husband has to say."

Together they moved toward the council ground. Once clear of the wagons they could see dismounted troopers strung out in a line across the creek. There didn't seem to be many more of them than comprised Lieutenant Milham's earlier details.

By the time they reached the meeting grounds, the crowd was half assembled. The wagon which Cap used as his rostrum at these meetings had been pushed out into the open and was being circled by the Boomers and their families. Racklin was watching Cap and the officer, who were standing by the wagon. Cap was speaking vehemently and the dark, stocky lieutenant was merely shaking his head in negation. Cap would talk and the lieutenant would refuse a reply.

Cap finally climbed up to the wagon bed and looked in all directions to see if more people were coming. The last few stragglers trotted to the edge of the crowd.

Now Cap raised both arms in his familiar command for silence.

"My friends, we have the Army with us again, as some of you can see. I have endeavored to learn from their commanding officer, Lieutenant June, what the Army wants with us. He has refused to tell me his business, but I can guess it. So can you." He paused, pitchman style, to isolate for effectiveness what he was to say next.

Again the arms went up. "I think Lieutenant June has the answer to the question he will ask us. Will we move? Let him hear your answer."

The crowd of Boomers roared "NO!" in angry chorus.

Cap's face beamed approval as his arms went up again, commanding silence. When he had it, he said, "Lieutenant June, will you step up here, please?" When Lieutenant June climbed into the wagon body, Cap said to the crowd, "This is Lieutenant June. Please hear him out."

June surveyed the silent crowd and then he said in a voice almost as carrying as Cap's, "I did not come here to ask a question. I came here to read an order from Headquarters, Department of the Missouri, United States Army. It reads as follows:

"To Major Kelso
Fort Reno
Indian Territory
    You are to call in from the field enough

227

men to constitute a full Troop. With this Troop you are ordered to isolate this aggregation of so-called Boomers from all supplies from the outside. This is to include staple foods and livestock of any description, including wild game. You are to forbid passage of all types of carrier vehicles to said camp. If a show of force is made, you are ordered to return in kind. If these trespassers agree to move peacefully, you are ordered to escort them back into the States.

　　By order: General Amos Chandler, Commander"

Lieutenant June's hand holding the paper dropped and before the crowd could react, he said, "For the information of you people, your camp was surrounded by troops yesterday evening."

Then a roar of protest welled up. Shouts of "Murderer!" "We'll starve!" "Damn the Army!" "Killers!" and like epithets were hurled at Lieutenant June who was pocketing his order. He paid the crowd no attention but stepped down from the wagon bed only to be replaced by Cap Frane who immediately raised his arms for silence. He did not get it immediately and he turned his head, arms still raised, to see Lieutenant June stalking through the crowd, headed for the creek.

"Lieutenant June!" Cap roared. "Come back here!" The shouting quieted the crowd but Lieutenant June paid no attention to Cap's orders.

"Seize that man!" Cap shouted. "Hold him! Bring him back here!"

Lieutenant June did not alter his pace and the men in front of him, in spite of Cap's orders, did not put a hand on him. Rather, they moved aside. There was something of finality about Lieutenant June's orders and his actions that told the Boomers that they were up against a reality they never thought they would have to face.

At the edge of the crowd, Lieutenant June mounted his horse and rode toward the creek without ever looking back.

Within a week's time five more council meetings had been called, but more than council meetings took place. Chickens which were so important to the Boomers as a source of food began to disappear, either eaten or stolen to eat. The first milk cow was killed and butchered and its meat dried. Some of this meat was boldly stolen from the drying racks. Mushrooms as a staple of diet began to appear. In that week the first Boomer, a cobbler who planned to lease space in the McLarens' big mercantile house, packed up his family and headed back for Kansas.

Supplies of everything besides food were short. The blacksmith was out of both fuel and iron and a broken tool stayed broken. Many people were sick because of the diet forced upon them by the circumstances. Those gardens which had been planted early were devastated. Angry freighters dumped their goods behind the Army pickets, then walked in to demand payment for goods the Boomers could not receive. One of the McLaren brothers received a sound thrashing from one of his contract teamsters, but the most exquisite torture was reserved for Will Racklin. He was almost out of whiskey.

As the Boomer camp was off limits to the troopers, some of the more enterprising Boomers bought Racklin's whiskey and traded it to the troopers for their rations. Thus Racklin was confronted with a seller's market with nothing to sell.

Another council meeting was called for this morning and looking out at the drizzling rain, Racklin wondered if it would be postponed. The meeting really didn't matter since its course was predictable. Those Boomers who had made a business contract with Cap Frane would again maintain that Cap had not delivered the homesteads he promised. Therefore, their money should be returned. Cap, on the other hand, would maintain that he had kept the bargain and that the Boomers, if they were forced to move, should sue the government for damages done them.

The triangle clanged now and Racklin knew the meeting was on, but he saw no reason for attending it. He had paid Cap money for the privilege of making a lot more money, so he had no complaint. Right now, he had his whiskey to dilute with water, and he set about doing it. Already there were complaints that a pint of his whiskey wouldn't even give a child the hiccups, but Racklin was in the enviable position of a gambler who runs the only game in town. He had the only whiskey and he wasn't forcing anyone to drink it.

With his whiskey bottled, he started for the plank bar and the case under it, when Catherine Henry, a shawl over her dark hair against the drizzle, appeared in the tent doorway.

"Come in, come in, Mrs. Frane," Racklin said in a jeering tone of voice.

Catherine stepped into the tent, took the shawl from her head and without being invited sat down in Racklin's chair. "That's a tired joke by now," Catherine said. "I wish you'd give it a rest."

Racklin regarded her closely. Like the majority of the Boomers now she seemed both tired and discouraged. "How come you ain't standing out there in the rain holding the Messiah's hand?"

"I already know what he'll say," Catherine said wearily. "We went over it at breakfast."

"No refund to the downtrodden farmers?"

"That's about it."

Now Racklin asked drily, "He has no money for the poor downtrodden grave-robber?"

Catherine looked at him in anger, but said nothing and her silence seemed to goad Racklin further.

Now his tone was mocking as he said, "Seriously, Catherine, I worry about you. You've led the Prince of Sod-busters into believing you'll marry him. You're honor-bound to, of course, but what's happening to his sod palace? What's happening to his choice business lots in this thriving hick community? What will happen to those widow's weeds that you're sewing on now?"

Then to Racklin's utter consternation, Catherine Henry buried her face in her hands and began to cry.

Racklin regarded her for a moment and her racking sobs smothered his muttered, "What the hell?" He moved over to her and awkwardly placed a hand on her shoulder. "I'm sorry I got so rough."

Soon the worst of the tears were over and

Catherine dabbed at her eyes with her shawl. "No, I deserve to be called a scheming bitch. That's what I was. It's what I am, too, because now I don't want to marry Cap. I was after money and now that he's broke, I don't want him."

"Your tears are for the gone money, then?"

"Only part of them," Catherine said slowly. "It wouldn't have been much of a marriage, Will, but it would have been something. I'd have been needed. I guess no man understands how necessary that is to a woman."

"You're needed," Racklin said quietly.

"By Ed and Mary? No. They don't need me. They tolerate me."

Racklin shook his head. "You damned fool," he said roughly. "Where're your eyes? I need you."

Catherine looked up at him, her lips parted in disbelief.

Racklin continued in a sober voice, "Why do you think I've been jabbing you about the old boy? I wanted to shame you out of making a play for him. Why did I want to? Because I didn't want Cap to get you."

Catherine found her voice now. "Why, Will Racklin, what are you saying?"

"You're a schemer. You're greedy, and you're lonely. I'm all of those things, too, Catherine. What I'm saying is, I want to marry you."

"You don't, Will. You're just sorry for me."

Now the bray came back into Racklin's voice. "Goddamn it, woman! I'm sorry for myself!" He said more gently, "Look. We're going to have to leave here. I've got money and I can win more in any of these railroad towns. It won't be much of a life, but I'll guarantee you we'll laugh, and likely half the time at each other."

Catherine smiled. "I'll think about it, Will."

Racklin shook his head. "Just do one thing in your life without having to scheme about it. You were willing to marry an old man without love. Marry me without love."

"If I said yes, I'd feel so cheap, Will."

"You are cheap. So am I. What's that got to do with it? Give a plain answer to a plain question, will you?"

"Yes."

It wasn't until they asked the hostler at the livery stable the name of this town that Milham was sure this was Alma. They found him in the light of the archway lantern holding the reins of the fresh stage team and when Milham asked him if he would put up their horses, he nodded laconically.

"Be about ten minutes." He tilted his head toward the tie rail. "Leave your horses there."

Milham and Nathan swung out of their

saddles and stretched. Milham's mustache blended into the beard stubble of his face, and now he took off his hat and beat the dust out of it by slapping it against his knee.

"Ever hear of a Beth Majors in this town?" he asked.

The hostler turned his head and pointed down the street with his chin. "The house on the far side of the church is hers."

Milham nodded his thanks, then he and Nathan headed down the street together.

"You reckon that Diamond H rider was right? How do you hide anybody in a town this size?" Nathan asked.

"Well, there *is* a Beth Majors. Maybe Hovey is only using her as a post office."

"You still John Weaver?"

"I don't know. Let's look it over first. Let me do the talking and you can pick it up from what I say."

Milham was as puzzled as Nathan. They had known, of course, that Hovey was holding Silence in a town, yet this crossroads collection of buildings could scarcely be called a town. He had noted a bar with a hotel in its second story, a hardware store, blacksmith shop and livery stable and a few homes. How could a person be hidden here?

During their long days of riding to this place, they had speculated on Hovey's probable reaction when they confronted him. Would he accept the fact that his scheme had failed and that the Boomers weren't going to move and that, therefore, he might just as well turn over Silence to them? Or would he refuse to believe their story, certain in his knowledge that no man would put his personal affairs ahead of the safety of his child.

The house on the far side of the church had a lamp alight by a window in the middle of the house; the front and back rooms were darkened.

"Somebody going to bed?" Nathan asked.

"Not quite yet," Milham said drily, and he led the way up the boardwalk onto the steps and across the porch. The door was open to catch the night breeze. Surely, Milham thought with pessimism, if Silence were being held here, the door would be locked. He knocked thunderously on the door frame.

From inside the house the husky voice of a woman called, "Who's that?"

"I'm looking for Beth Majors," Milham called back.

"She's out of town. Now go away."

Milham looked at Nathan, but it was too dark to see his reaction. He called then, "Can you come to the door? This is important."

Beth Majors called back, "I'm sick in bed. Now go away."

Milham swiftly made up his mind. He touched Nathan on the elbow and then stepped into the house and Nathan followed. They crossed the room, heading for the light thrown from a doorway in the hallway opposite. Milham entered the hall and turned right, halting in the doorway of a bedroom. In the far corner was a bed that held the shapeless bulk of a red-haired woman. She could have been in her forties, Milham thought, but if so, every one of those years had been hard ones, as was reflected in her lined and cynical face. On the coverlet was spread out a game of patience and now with the hand that held the cards, she closed her wrapper in a gesture of modesty.

"Say, who the hell do you think you are?" Beth snarled. "You can't walk in my house like that. Get out of here!"

"We were told this was Beth Majors' house, but you claim it's yours."

"I'll claim anything I want! Will you get out of here before I call for help?"

"Then you are Beth Majors."

Milham took a step into the room to allow Nathan to enter. Now Beth threw back the covers, swung her feet to the floor and reached beyond the lamp on the bed table and drew down the shade. Then she returned to the bed and pulled the covers over her.

"If I am, who are you and what are you doing walking into my house with a damned Indian?"

"I was sent here by a Diamond H rider to find Jess Hovey."

A look of caution replaced the anger in Beth's face. "Look, Mister. You've either got the wrong name or the wrong town. I don't know anybody by the name of Jess Hovey."

"My name is John Weaver from Ithaca, New York," Milham said quietly. "I want to buy Hovey's grass lease and his cattle. I'm prepared to pay seventy-five thousand dollars for them."

Beth studied him in silence, and Milham could almost read what was going through her mind by the varied expressions on her face. First, there was skepticism, then calculation, then caution.

"You say a Diamond H rider sent you here?"

"Why would I be here if he didn't? I told him my business. He said I could find Jess Hovey here."

There was another long wait as Beth studied him. "I may be able to put you in touch with him," she said finally.

"Then you are Beth Majors and you do know Jess Hovey and he's here. You've lied in answer to every question, but you better not lie to this one." He paused. "Where is she?"

"Who?"

"Silence Frane."

"Nobody's named that," Beth scoffed. Now an expression of manufactured anger came into her face. "Say, who are you? What do you want?"

"Silence Frane."

"Well, whoever or whatever that is, I ain't got it! Get out!" Suddenly Nathan bellowed at the top of his lungs, "Silence! Where are you?"

They listened and as they did, Beth's hand moved under the pillow. Dimly, then, they heard a sound as if a door was being pounded or kicked. They were both half-turned when Beth's snarling voice came to them. "Stand still!"

When they turned, they saw the six-gun in Beth's hand pointed at them. Slowly, she got out of bed, keeping them under her gun. When she spoke now, there was triumph in her voice. "Now handsome, you and that Injun step into the room. You shut the door."

Milham looked at Nathan and back at Beth and began to move. Nathan, however, made a motion as if to come forward, then whirled and lunged out into the dark hall.

Beth pulled the trigger. Milham felt, rather

than heard, the slug whomp into the door frame while the explosion of the gun in this small room almost deafened him. Now Milham listened, and he heard the sound of Nathan mounting the stairs as fast as his legs could drive him.

Beth was listening, too, her head cocked to one side. The floor overhead creaked and they could both hear Nathan calling, "Silence! Silence! Where are you?" Again came the pounding and now they heard Nathan speak. They could not make out what he said.

Suddenly there was a shot upstairs and they heard the sound of a door being kicked savagely.

Now a new sound, and from the front room, came to them. Milham turned in time to see Hovey halt in the doorway.

"There's another one upstairs, Jess. Hurry!"

"Keep him here," Hovey said, and disappeared down the hall.

Milham shouted, "Look out, Nathan!"

This was a resourceful woman, Milham thought, but she didn't know guns. As he moved forward, she raised the gun and pulled the trigger. Nothing happened, for it was a double action Colt and she had tried to shoot it without remembering to cock it.

Milham moved in and wrenched the gun from her. Ramming it in his waistband, he whirled and strode out into the hall. He could hear Hovey driving up the stairs. A sudden shot from upstairs boomed through the house and seemed to halt him on the stairs.

Feeling the wall in the darkness, Milham came to a corner, turned and found the stairway. Looking up it, he saw nothing but impenetrable blackness.

Crouching now, he started to inch his way up the stairs on all fours. He had no notion where Hovey was or if Hovey knew he was climbing after him.

Again, Milham heard the floor creak above him, then the sound of a squeaking hinge came to him. Suddenly, there was light from something burning at the top of the stairwell. It was followed by a shot.

Now Hovey, who had been flattened on the stairs, backed down, turned and started downstairs. He was a tall black shape, silhouetted against the light and now Milham lifted his gun; when he lost its sight in Hovey's blackness, he squeezed the trigger.

Hovey was rammed flat on his back by the slug from Milham's gun. His own gun fell from his hand as he hit the stairs and then he began to slide, half-turned on his side, then on his face, as his body gained momentum.

Milham stepped out of the way and Hovey came to rest at his feet.

Milham looked up, saw Nathan at the head of the stairwell stamping out a fire from a burning curtain that he had pulled down and lighted in order to see Hovey. Milham took the stairs two at a time and then, behind Nathan and to one side, was Silence, in the lamplight thrown from a room to her left. Her face looked bruised and swollen but nothing could hide the joy and relief that were reflected. Without a word, she moved over and hugged Nathan and then came to Milham and hugged him. By now, there were tears, for Milham felt them through his shirt as she buried her head against his chest.

Nathan stood out of the light so that even if Milham had been watching him, he could not have seen the fleeting expression of sadness that touched Nathan's face then.

"Let's get out of here," Nathan said. "We'll have the whole damn town on us."

Striking a match on the wall, Nathan led the way down the stairs, Silence following him, Milham following her. Hovey lay just as Milham had left him, on his face, and motionless in pooling blood.

Skirting him, they moved down the hall and halted at the bedroom door. Beth Majors sat on the edge of the bed, anger and bitterness in her ravaged face. Milham took her six-gun from his waistband, punched out the bullets, pocketed them, and tossed the gun on the bed.

"He's dead," Beth said dully.

Milham nodded. "Tell any story you want about how he died." He paused. "If it involves any of us, then get used to the idea of prison. That's where you'll go."

They moved on through the dark living room out into the night. Half a dozen men were gathered out on the street watching the house. As the three of them came down the boardwalk and turned up the street, a man called, "What happened in there?"

"I don't rightly know," Milham said. "Beth Majors is in there. Ask her."

Now Silence fell between Nathan and Milham and took each by the arm. "Bless you, bless you both," she said quietly.

Now Nathan halted, thus halting them. "Scott, there's rooms over the saloon. You take Silence there and I'll be along later. I want to find out what story that woman gives out."

"Hurry then, Nathan," Silence said.

Nathan nodded and moved a little closer to Silence as if trying to make out her features in the darkness. Then he raised his hand and touched her cheek and said, "Sure, Sis."

Milham and Silence went on and Nathan, standing in the middle of the street, watched them go. It was Scott who would have to tell

Silence of Cap's abandonment of her, but it wouldn't hurt her too deeply, Nathan thought. She had Scott to love and cherish her and that was really all that counted.

When he saw them reach the four corners, Nathan started off in their direction. When he was even with the livery stable, he turned into the livery office.

The hostler, sleeping on the cot in the office, roused and Nathan flipped him a silver dollar and said, "My horse is where?"

"Third stall on your left. Take the lantern."

Minutes later Nathan rode out alone, heading north into a country he hoped had never heard of Boomers.

The employees of THORNDIKE PRESS hope you have enjoyed this Large Print book. All our Large Print titles are designed for easy reading, and all our books are made to last. Other Thorndike Large Print books are available at your library, through selected bookstores, or directly from us. For more information about current and upcoming titles, please call or mail your name and address to:

THORNDIKE PRESS
PO Box 159
Thorndike, Maine 04986
800/223-6121
207/948-2962